Praise for Dana Marie Bell's
Shadow of the Wolf

"Magical in more ways than one, this story is worth reading."

~ *Night Owl Reviews*

"Exciting and fast moving, *Shadow of the Wolf* is pure entertainment and a joy to read. A true keeper!"

~ *The Romance Studio*

"The first story in the *Heart's Desire* series was both humorous and a good suspense story... Ms. Bell is a new author for me and I am looking forward to more about the Beckett family..."

~ *Literary Nymphs Reviews*

"I loved *Shadow of the Wolf*...it isn't just the explicit sex that burn up the pages that holds you, it's the romantic gestures and warm family feelings that clue you into the characters' hearts."

~ *Fresh Fiction*

Look for these titles by
Dana Marie Bell

Now Available:

Shadow of the Wolf

Dana Marie Bell

Samhain Publishing, Ltd.
11821 Mason Montgomery Road, 4B
Cincinnati, OH 45249
www.samhainpublishing.com

Shadow of the Wolf
Copyright © 2013 by Dana Marie Bell
Print ISBN: 978-1-61921-363-0
Digital ISBN: 978-1-61921-095-0

Editing by Tera Kleinfelter
Cover by Lyn Taylor

First Samhain Publishing, Ltd. electronic publication: September 2012
First Samhain Publishing, Ltd. print publication: August 2013

Dedication

To Mom, who still makes me call her to make sure I arrived to and from conventions safely. I may be [CENSORED] years old, but I'll always be your baby, even if you tell people you're dad's much younger bride who adopted his children after we were already grown.

(Can I have my cookie now? No? Damn.)

To Dad, who I'm pretty sure will have a love-hate relationship with Diablo III when he finally gets around to picking it up. What, no paladin class? GASP! The wizard rocks, though. Wizards *always* rock.

And to Dusty, who makes every day magical.

Prologue

Christopher stared down at his preparations, mentally checking and rechecking each and every one. All of the runes were aligned properly within the circle, spelling out his intent. The incense was burning sweetly, its cinnamon scent filling the air and making him think of home. The small fire he'd created in his cauldron burned merrily. Colored candles were lit and placed in the proper alignment. A rose for love and an iris for wisdom, stems braided through an emerald ring sacred to Venus and used for this purpose for generations, waited for him to begin the chant. Every item held a piece of the spell. The words would merely cement it, bringing the pieces of his magical puzzle together into one cohesive picture that would send his call out into the world.

Everything was as it should be. Not one single thing was out of place or forgotten.

He took a deep breath, mentally placing himself in the frame of mind necessary to cast the spell. This was it, one of the defining moments of his life. His ancestor's spell would determine the course of the rest of his life. He closed his eyes, concentrating on his perfect mate. She should be of an older lineage, someone born from power, with magic to complement his own. She should be petite. Christopher had a fondness for women who were smaller than he was. Hair and eye color didn't matter to him, though he had a preference for blondes. And she needed to have an open mind, to be able to accept the one thing setting him apart from most other wizards.

He was so very tired of being alone. Not even his brothers could ease the loneliness that had begun to plague him. He fingered the blue piece of paper waiting for the fire and visualized everything he hoped for. Everything his soul cried out for.

He could feel the power building within him. He'd written down his wishes in red ink, the color of passion, ready to be burned in the cauldron.

It was time.

Christopher reached into the pocket of his purple silk robe and pulled out a wand crafted of oak, especially created just for this ritual. He slipped the sheet into the flames, watching it catch fire before dropping it into the cauldron. Raising his arms high, he began his chant. As the paper burned, he concentrated with every ounce of will he had on the meaning behind the words. Without intent, the words would be useless, gibberish muttered in the dark.

"I call on forces higher than I,

To awaken the dreams I hold inside.

Venus, grant me the love I lack;

With this spell my mate attract!

This candle for her,

This candle for me.

When they touch,

United we'll be.

Kindle the love,

Kindle the flame,

When we meet, she'll know my name.

By the power of earth and fire,

Bring unto me my heart's desire.

By the power of air and sea,

As I will so mote it be."

As he chanted, two candles, both red, one carved with the symbol of female, the other marked with the symbol for male and bearing a lock of his hair, shifted slightly toward one another. Christopher fought his smile.

The ritual was working.

Abruptly the candles stopped. He repeated the chant two more times, invoking the power of three, and felt the spell settle in his bones. The last of the paper burned to ash in a puff of red smoke, and Christopher smiled triumphantly.

It had worked. His mate was coming to him. He would watch the candles. When they touched, he would begin scrying for his mate, using the clear crystal globe on his desk to show her image to him. Alasdair would alert him when she came close to his property, passing the detection wards he had in place. Now all he had to do was wait for her.

He snorted, amused now that the spell was done. He'd always waited for her and hadn't known it until the howling loneliness threatened to engulf him. It had taken a long talk with his father to show him exactly what was happening and what he could do to fix it. Once he'd touched the emerald ring, all other possible options were put aside in favor of the one he knew would work.

He needed the other half of his soul to finally be complete.

He carefully extinguished the red candles, watched until the flames in the cauldron slowly died down. The incense he allowed to burn, enjoying the scent of cinnamon. The runes and symbols he left untouched. He would perform no other works until his mate was at his side.

With a yawn and a satisfied smile, Christopher pulled off his robe and hung it neatly on the peg by the door. It was late, just past midnight, and he was in dire need of a run. He always felt pleasantly tired after finishing a spell, like he'd given both his body and his mind a good workout. Running would ease any last, lingering tension left behind, leaving him pleasantly relaxed and ready for bed.

Opening the back door, he quickly reactivated the wards against intruders. He stripped off his pants, shirt, shoes and socks, and laid them carefully on the glass-topped table on his stone patio. With a sigh of relief, he allowed the change to take him, shaking his coat in primal joy. His mate would be here soon, and he would no longer be a lone wolf.

He ran into the darkness of the woods, unaware that the two candles had begun to slide closer together.

Chapter One

Lana banged her head repeatedly against the steering wheel of her car, muttering under her breath. She turned the key for the umpteenth time with a swift prayer to the Lady. Again, nothing happened, not even the grinding sound of the starter. Her poor little Beetle had up and died in the middle of the night on a deserted highway, with a thunderstorm threatening to break over her head.

Wonderful. I get to be a cliché.

It wouldn't be the first time her car had broken down, and it probably wouldn't be the last, although she could honestly say this was probably the *worst* time her car had ever chosen to stop running. *I really should just give up and get a new car.* Kerry, her best friend, had mentioned it that night at the bridal shower, but she'd once again brushed off Kerry's concerns over the clunker Lana drove. Usually when the Bug died on her she was able to get it up and running again with a quick call to AAA and a stop at the mechanic's. *Not an option in East Bumblefuck, PA, at two o'clock in the morning.* Keeping the Bug running was usually a labor of love.

Nothing quite like unrequited love, is there?

She knew she wasn't out of gas, because she'd filled up just before leaving the small town the Naughty Nights Club had been in. It couldn't be the alternator. She'd just replaced that.

And the starter was only six months old. The car had died while running, so it couldn't be the battery. Could it?

Lana wasted a moment wishing Kerry had followed her, but her friend had been flirting with a very hot male stripper, and Lana hadn't wanted to interrupt. If she'd known that the small spike of unease she'd felt just before heading out would lead to a broken-down car in the middle of freaking nowhere, she would have plastered herself to Kerry's side.

Damn it. No matter how badly she wanted to, she couldn't just "zap" the Beetle. She stood a good chance of doing even more damage that way. Magically fixing anything mechanical usually ended in a disaster of epic proportions, especially since she had a bad tendency to get angry when it didn't work. Anger and witchcraft just didn't mix well.

And why the fuck had Kelly, Kerry's twin, picked some place so far off the beaten path to have her bachelorette party anyway? Who heard of a male strip club so far out in the boondocks? *Kelly the Crazy, that's who.* She'd badgered Kerry about it until Kerry had thrown her hands up and made the arrangements, but Lana knew Kerry. Kerry had some sort of revenge planned for her sweet, annoying twin.

She'd been right. Lana just hoped Kelly's fiancé didn't get wind of the lap dance Kerry had bought for her, because odds were good it wouldn't be Kelly who got into trouble. Dennis and Kerry got along about as well as dogs and fleas. Kerry *lived* to annoy the straight-arrow Dennis, and Dennis tolerated Kerry only for Kelly's sake.

One thing she could say about the man, he *did* love Kelly more than anyone or anything. The happiness Kerry saw in her twin's eyes made Kerry much more pleasant than she could have been toward the man. The last guy Kelly had dated hadn't fared nearly so well. Kerry'd put an entire fifteen-ounce bottle of

Jean Naté after-bath splash into the man's Listerine.

It had gone downhill from there. Kerry had the pictures to prove it.

A shock of thunder caused her to jump. With a sigh, she pulled out her cell phone. Hopefully she'd be able to get a tow truck despite the storm and the late hour. Hell, if Kerry was still available, maybe Lana could pry her away from the prime beef she'd been plastered to long enough to lend a hand.

She flipped the phone open and stared at the distinct lack of phonage. *How could the battery be dead? The stupid thing was plugged in!* Lana made sure to keep it on the car charger... She fumbled around, finally finding the end of the cord in the pitch black car. *Well, shit.* The plug was loose in the outlet. It may have been on the charger, but it sure hadn't been charging.

Isn't this the part where the spooky music is supposed to start?

With a weary groan, Lana opened her door. The heavens opened up above her, pouring rain down on her outstretched arm, soaking it in seconds. *Oh yeah. Cue the music.* All the night needed was a scary black figure at the end of the road.

She glanced in the rearview mirror, unable to help herself. *Road clear, thank the Goddess.*

Reaching into her back seat, she pulled out her umbrella. Of course, it refused to open. When she finally forced it open, the wind plucked it right out of her hands and sent it flying into the dark, wet night.

Lana glared up into the storm. "Are you trying to tell me something? I mean, you've got my attention."

Lightning, quickly followed by thunder, answered her.

No car, no phone, no umbrella, and a nice long walk to the strip joint in the pouring rain. Maybe I should stay put and wait for a cop. Isn't that what they say to do if your car breaks down? And isn't that what I'd yell at the screen right about now?

Of course, I'd also be thinking that the poor girl was pretty much toast either way. Especially if this was the beginning of the movie, 'cause that would mean I wasn't the heroine. She *wasn't the heroine. Whatever.*

Once again, lightning and thunder answered her. There was a definite *Move!* vibe to the air that had her instincts howling at her much like the wind was. And one thing Lana always did was listen to her instincts.

She glanced around the dark interior of the car. *Because this is what happens when I don't.* Thunder rumbled overhead, ominous, the air heavy with the threat of the next lightning strike.

Okay, okay, I get the message!

Lana grabbed her purse and keys and got out of her car. She started walking, heading away from the nightclub. Why she was being prodded in the opposite direction she had no clue, but she was done ignoring the fates tonight. With any luck the powers that be would eventually let her know where she was going, but she wasn't about to hold her breath. Apparently she'd done *something* to piss off the Karma police. She just hoped her punishment was nothing worse than a bad cold.

Christopher returned from an early evening run, refreshed and oddly jubilant. He loved running in the woods, but tonight somehow felt different.

He felt his familiar's tug when he crossed the boundaries of his property. He stepped, naked and human, onto the back porch. Reaching for the jeans he'd left on the glass-topped patio

16

table, he stopped at Alasdair's meow. The heavens opened up and drenched him before he could even finish unfolding them. Shivering in the cooler air, he quickly abandoned the damp jeans and stepped into the house.

Alasdair appeared, his tail quivering high in the air. He rubbed himself against Christopher's calf before running toward the crystal Christopher used for scrying. A quick peek into his workroom showed that the two candles were finally touching.

After a month of waiting, his mate was finally here.

Christopher sat at his desk, swallowing to calm himself. She was here, within his reach. For the first time in his life his hands were shaking from nerves. He stared at the crystal ball, eager to finally see his mate. All of the preparation spells for scrying where already long in place, just requiring an activation spell. With a wave of his hand, he muttered,

"By the power of earth and fire,

Show to me my heart's desire.

By the power of air and sea,

As I will so mote it be."

Mist swirled briefly within the ball, clearing abruptly. Christopher's eyes widened when he saw his chosen mate for the first time.

Goddess, she's beautiful.

But the more he watched, the more he knew something was very, very wrong.

Lana slogged through the woods, grumpy as hell. She'd followed the road for about half a mile before the urge to leave it had overcome her. Following her instincts she'd gone to the right, into the woods, rather than to the left, where the ground

17

was more open. Something felt very wrong about being in the open right now, something that would leave her...vulnerable. Enough so that she was willing to go into a wooded area during a thunderstorm.

Not your brightest move to date. If the lightning didn't get her, whatever was hunting her would.

She was thoroughly soaked. Her boots squished when she walked, her hair was a bedraggled mess, and she knew her mascara was running down her face. She wiped the moisture away, not that it did any good. With any luck she'd strike just the right note of pathetic to get some help. Hopefully someone was nearby who would take pity on such a sucky night and give her a hand. Or a phone. Or a hand holding a phone.

Hell, while we're wishing for miracles, a cup of hot chocolate would be nice too.

Lana shivered, her teeth chattering in the cold autumn rain. Her booted feet kept slipping on the wet leaves, the three-inch heels definitely not meant for hiking in rain-drenched forests. She was lucky she hadn't broken her ankle yet, but she had to keep moving. Her internal trouble radar was pinging like mad, urging her forward, her fear spiking until all she wanted to do was *run.*

She was being hunted.

She didn't hear, or see, a thing, but she *knew* something was behind her.

Something meant to hurt her.

Why didn't I hear the spooky music, damn it?

She picked up her pace, but running was out of the question. It was black as pitch, and her night vision was bad on the brightest nights. Tonight she couldn't see a thing except during those brief flashes of lightning. The rain, wind and thunder muffled any sounds she might have heard, so tracking her stalker that way was impossible.

Whatever chased her was keeping pace if the way her instincts were howling was anything to go by. She considered throwing up a witchlight but the damn thing would be a beacon to whoever was behind her.

When the fifth branch in fifteen minutes smacked her in the face, Lana started to mutter under her breath. She clutched her purse to her, her eyes wide and afraid. She searched the darkness around her, even more certain she was being hunted.

And then she felt it. A second presence. There was someone nearby, someone who could help. Her instincts were never wrong. Two people stalked her in the night. One meant safety, the other did not. Now she just had to figure out which one was which.

Guessing wrong would be very, very bad.

Christopher watched his mate pick up speed, her face full of fear. He felt the sense she had of being stalked, and it worried him.

Could Cole be out there? Would Cole have sensed Christopher's call for his mate? Would Cole hurt Christopher's mate just to challenge him?

Christopher couldn't take that chance. With a last, lingering glance at the dark-haired female, he stalked to the back porch. He glared at the rain-drenched yard and changed shape with a shudder.

He hated getting rained on.

He darted into the night, his wolf eyes much more suited to the darkness than the man's had been. Sniffing the wind, he quickly found the scent of the female. *His* female, *his* mate. And something else, something elusive, something that stalked her. Something familiar that he hadn't smelled in a long time.

Cole.

The wolf paused, growling, sifting through the scents and the sounds. His woman smelled incredibly delicious. Baked apples and warm sunshine, she tugged on his senses in a way he hadn't expected. He moved swiftly and silently through the damp forest, that wonderful scent leading him straight to his prey. He stopped in front of her, confident he was hidden in the dark trees.

Soaking wet jeans molded to one of the finest asses it had ever been his pleasure to see. High-heeled black boots slipped and slid on the wet leaves, nearly landing her on said ass. He couldn't tell what size her breasts were because of the bulky knit poncho she wore, but if they matched her ass, she'd be a truly pleasant handful. Her hair lay plastered to her skull, the color impossible to tell. Porcelain skin glowed even in the dark night. She tried to blow a strand of wet hair out of her eyes, rolling said eyes with such impatience that the man inside the wolf grinned.

There you are.

Chapter Two

Lana stopped, a strange sense of both safety and vulnerability flashing through her. *That way.* She started to turn to her left and shrieked.

Lightning flashed, thunder rumbled, and the dark shape of a man stood before her. His eyes gleamed in the flash of lightning, his grin triumphant. He reached out toward her and tried to grab her arm.

Her entire being shuddered away from him. Lana stepped away from the man. "Why have you been following me?"

The man tilted his head. "Isn't your car broken down on the road? I thought you could use some help."

His voice was a pleasant blend of concern and attraction. Lana's eyes narrowed, bringing up her second sight. Usually she could conjure up a person's aura fairly easily, but this man's was somehow shielded. Unfortunately she got just enough of a feel off of that shield to know what she was dealing with.

Damn. A freaking wizard. Figures.

No way did she want to engage in a magical dance with a wizard, especially when she couldn't tell how strong he was. Lana took a step back. Every instinct she had pushing her away from the man in front of her.

"I'd be careful too. There are rumors of some kind of wild animal in these parts. Found a few dogs mangled in the woods."

The concern in his voice was false. A flash of black and sickly green surrounded him, the colors murky and muddled, before he shielded himself once more. Something was off about those colors, but she was too cold and tired to figure it out now. "Ah, thanks for the warning." Lana took another step away from the scary stranger, her instincts screaming at her that her only safety lay *behind* her, somewhere in the shadows.

The man matched her, moving forward a step. "You really should have waited in your car for a cop or something, Miss...?"

Lana put her hands behind her, feeling for trees and branches. She continued to move away from the menace she sensed in front of her. If she could reach the safe harbor she felt behind her, everything would be all right.

Only if she could reach it, though.

Then again, the Lord does help those who help themselves. Her eyes were drawn to the branch swaying dangerously above his head. *And the Lady provides the means.*

The stranger dropped all pretense of helpfulness. He shook his head at her, his expression annoyed. "Are you going to make this difficult? It doesn't have to be painful, you know."

"What doesn't have to be painful?"

"Your death."

With those words several things happened at once. A long, menacing growl erupted out of the darkness. One of the shadows hurtled through the night, knocking the blond man onto his ass.

And the branch he'd been standing under snapped, helped along by Lana and the force of the wind, hitting the blond on the top of his head and knocking him out cold.

The shadow animal turned, its golden eyes trained on Lana. Slowly it stalked toward her, its body moving with a supple, lethal grace.

A black wolf. In rural Pennsylvania.

Lord? Lady? No freaking way that's *safe.* Lana gulped, and wondered if, somewhere out there, Fate was laughing its ass off at her.

Christopher's heart was still pounding in his chest. He turned toward his mate, scenting her for any injuries. He relaxed a bit when all he smelled were scratches, most likely from her flight through the woods.

When Cole had threatened her, it had been all he could do not to rip out the bastard's throat. The only thing that had saved him had been the falling branch and his mate's horrified gasp.

She was brave, his female. She stood there and watched him coming toward her with big, chocolate brown eyes wide with fear and...

Yes. Fascination. Good. Much better than the fear he'd sensed coursing through her as Cole threatened her.

He approached her slowly, his eyes never leaving hers. When he reached her side, he gently stroked her thigh with his massive head, unable to prevent the rough, happy grumble that leapt to his throat.

"Oh boy."

Her soft whisper sent shivers down his spine. His tail curled in pleasure, waving back and forth. Her hand came to rest tentatively on his broad back, her fingers digging into his fur.

With a yip he turned. Gently he gathered her hand in his

mouth, careful of his sharp teeth, and tugged her toward his home.

"Um, okay. Go with the big doggie. Got it."

He rolled his eyes but did his best to ignore her words. The breathy, scared tone of voice matched her scent—frightened, wary and brave. Christopher felt pride in his mate. She followed his lead, barely sparing Cole a glance. It pleased him that she made no move to give his enemy aid.

Certain now she followed, Christopher let her hand go and stalked into the cold, wet night.

I'm following a wolf through the woods in rural Pennsylvania after it attacked a man who told me he was going to kill me, and somehow my inner warning signal is okay with that.

Lana pinched the fleshy part of her arm hard. "OW!"

The wolf stopped and looked at her curiously, its head tilted to the side.

"Nope, not dreaming." Lana rubbed at her arm, hoping it wouldn't bruise. She hadn't meant to pinch quite *that* hard.

The wolf huffed and turned, heading off once more. Of the two strangers she'd met in the woods tonight, Lana considered the wolf far less dangerous, at least to her. The way the big wolf had acted after she'd hit the man on the head with that branch had been surreal, but not very frightening at all. The sense of safety she'd been heading toward had centered itself on the wolf, and she'd felt compelled to follow wherever he led.

The big wolf led her through the woods, his footfalls silent and sure. The few times she lost sight of the wolf he returned, tugging on her hand to lead her forward.

I hope wherever we're going I can take my boots off. My feet are killing me.

"Are we there yet?"

Up ahead the wolf gave a strange chuffing cough.

"And I'm sure I'd understand that if I spoke fluent woof."

The wolf stopped, staring at her again. "What?"

The wolf gave a shake of his head before moving forward once again.

"Yup, you're male."

Once again that proud head turned toward her. She could almost sense the question he wanted to ask.

"You haven't once stopped for directions and you don't make a lick of sense."

Those golden eyes narrowed, almost as if... *Nah. Not possible.* Grammy had told her a long time ago that shapeshifters were a myth. *Although he could be someone's familiar. That would explain how he seems to understand me.* But even familiars didn't have the level of intelligence this wolf seemed to possess, unless he was under a compulsion spell of some kind.

And anyone who put a compulsion spell on someone else wasn't someone she wanted to meet.

She felt the magical barriers before they passed through them, early enough that she stopped before going in. "Wait."

The wolf, on the other side of the barrier, yipped impatiently.

"No way. I have no clue what's on the other side. For all I know you actually work for tall, blond and dorky. You could be luring me into his evil lair." Not that she actually believed that, but for some reason her instincts were telling her that crossing that border meant nothing would ever be the same again. She wasn't certain yet if it was a good thing or a bad thing, since her insides were currently filled with butterflies doing a crazy, half-scared, half-excited mambo.

The wolf lowered his dark head, golden eyes closed. She could almost hear the pleas for patience.

Guess that answers that question. A familiar, then. At least she knew for certain now she was dealing with someone magical. "Besides, judging from the look and feel, whoever's on the other side is a wizard." The wolf's head snapped up. "Not sure I'm so eager to meet up with another one of those any time soon." The wolf slowly shook his head. "Well, what would you do if you were in my—" she looked down at her feet, "—boots?"

The wolf snorted.

"Yes, I know, Pup in Boots, doggie drag, call it what you will. The question remains. Would you put your life into an unknown wizard's hands?"

The image of the wolf blurred until a tall, wet, *naked* man stood in front of her.

"You already did."

Lana blinked. Her mouth opened, but nothing came out, other than a whimpered "Ugh."

The man's lips twitched. "Are you coming through or do you like getting rained on?"

Lana squeaked.

Hot, wet, naked male, with dark hair and golden eyes. *Golden* eyes.

The same eyes as the wolf who'd led her through the forest.

Sorry, Grammy, looks like you were wrong.

The man's mouth curved up into a sensuous smile. "Of course this would be a great deal more fun if you were also naked."

"Guh."

He held out his hand. "Come to me."

Lana hesitated. There was something about his stance, about the way he phrased the command, that worried her. There was something *irrevocable* about it, and she suddenly wanted to make a run for her dead car.

The smile left his face. Determination hardened his features, as if he sensed her hesitation. "Come to me."

The whispered seduction of his voice wrapped around her, teasing her senses, tugging her forward until she crossed the barrier, mambo-dancing butterflies be damned.

Well, fuck. Looks like I get to dance with a wizard after all.

Chapter Three

Christopher could barely contain his excitement. His mate was standing outside his home, staring up at the lit windows cautiously, her dark eyes somber. She was shivering with the cold, soaked to the bone and still stubbornly refusing to enter. "Come inside."

"Said the spider to the fly."

He would have found it amusing if her teeth weren't chattering and her lips weren't blue. "You're soaked to the skin and freezing. Would you rather stay outside and run the risk of getting sick, or would you like to come inside and get dry?" He would force the issue if she tried to remain outside, consequences be damned.

She studied him warily before nodding grudgingly. She stepped over the threshold and into the warmth of the house.

He pointed toward the floor. "Strip. Drop your clothes there. I'll be back in a moment with blankets and towels."

She actually growled at him before tugging off the poncho.

Satisfied that she was following his commands, he turned away, heading into the laundry room for some clean towels. He hadn't had a chance yet to fold laundry that evening, and now he was grateful for it. He toweled himself off and tugged on a pair of jeans, hoping that covering himself would make her more comfortable in his home.

He strode into the kitchen and froze, every single thought driven out of his head. She stood there clad only in simple white cotton, but that cotton was drenched, clinging to her skin like the finest silk. He could see the dusky color of her nipples through the cloth, the thatch of dark hair at the apex of her thighs.

One hand went to cover the sweet triangle between her thighs, the other reaching up to cover her breasts. "Towel. Please."

He stalked toward her, putting every ounce of seduction he knew into it, gratified to see her fingers trembling from more than the cold when she took the towel from him. "Follow me."

He didn't wait to see if she obeyed him. He led her farther into the house, toward the fireplace in his great room. With a wave of his hand and a few muttered words, he lit a roaring blaze guaranteed to warm her through.

The crystal ball wasn't the only pre-programmed spell in the house.

"Great."

He turned to find her glaring at him. He reached behind her to the sofa, pulling the off a blanket draped over the back and wrapping it around her shoulders. "What's great?"

"Nothing."

He could feel one of his eyebrows trying to climb into his hairline. "Why does that tone bother me?"

"You're the wizard. You figure it out."

He settled on the rug in front of the fireplace. "Why do I get the feeling you're prejudiced against wizards?" *And why do I suddenly think you aren't one?* A thought he hadn't entertained. After all, he'd asked for another wizard for a mate.

Hadn't he?

"Maybe because wizards are prejudiced against me." She settled on the opposite side of the fireplace, her expression wary. He would have to see what he could do to remedy that.

But for now he would deal with the first issue. "Why would wizards be prejudiced against you?"

She licked her lips, and everything male in him stood at attention. He didn't hear her reply, too focused on what that pink tongue would feel like lapping at the head of his now aching cock.

"Hello!" The snapping of her fingers brought his attention to the rest of her face. "Do I want to know what you were thinking just now?"

"Do you like chocolate syrup?"

She blinked. "What?"

"Do you like chocolate syrup?"

"Uh, no?"

"Then no."

The wary look was back in her eyes. "Alrighty then. Can I borrow your phone?"

"Borrow my phone? Why?"

"To call for someone to come and pick me up, obviously."

When hell freezes over. "Perhaps after we're dry?"

"I could have them bring over clothes. And I need someone to take a look at my car. It broke down on the road, and why am I telling a complete stranger all this? You could be an axe murderer."

He laughed. "I'm not, I promise."

"I'm sure all axe murderers say that right before they break out the axe."

He snorted, thoroughly amused. She was snuggling deeper

into the blanket, the heat warming her through, her teeth chattering less and less. "Getting a tow truck out here during this storm would be a true feat of magic."

She sighed and propped her chin on her hand, looking forlorn. He wanted to snatch her up and cuddle her close, but there was no way she was ready. "True."

"Perhaps I could take a look at your car after the storm passes."

"Perhaps you could." She jumped when Alasdair landed in her lap. "Oh!" She reached out and tentatively petted Alasdair, a delighted smile on her face. Alasdair, the shameless thing, purred in obvious delight before settling down. "Your familiar?"

He nodded, hoping his pet would put her at ease in a way Christopher seemed incapable of doing. She seemed to like the cat, and Alasdair certainly seemed to like her. It was always a good thing when your familiar liked your mate. Chris shuddered thinking about the mischief Alasdair could get up to if he'd taken a dislike to her.

She opened her mouth, her brow furrowed, before shaking her head and clamping her lips closed.

"Go ahead and ask. I promise I won't bite yet."

"Yet?"

He merely smiled. She'd find out sooner rather than later if he had any say in the matter.

"How did you...? I mean, Grammy said that shapeshifters were a myth."

He watched her, the play of emotions over her heart-shaped face. "They are."

"Then, how?"

"How do I become the wolf?" She nodded. "Simple. I'm—"

"Christopher Beckett." Her eyes widened in shock.

31

He grinned, unable to hold back the feral satisfaction and deep longing to finalize the cementing of their bond. *She knows my name. It really is her.* "Yes."

She shook her head. "How did I know that?"

He needed a diversion. It was too soon to give that part of the game away. "Would you like some hot chocolate?" The wistful hunger on her face drove him to his feet. "Enjoy the fire. I'll return momentarily." He didn't want his new mate catching cold before he'd had a chance to claim her. "Don't move. I don't want you getting sick." Besides, he planned on adding a little something that would ensure she'd still be there come morning.

Lana moved her legs, thinking perhaps it would be better to grab her wet clothes and make for the hills, but the warm weight of the purring cat held her in place. Deep gold-green eyes slitted open, staring up at her with lazy arrogance, daring her to move.

"Like master like familiar, huh?"

Speaking of the master, how in the hell had she known the man's name? Something was going on here, and it had her magic senses tingling. The thing was, instead of blaring the warning she expected, they were, well, *tingling.* She couldn't get the image of him standing there, naked, half-hard cock dangling between his thighs, his hand held out, his deep, purring voice demanding that she come to him. And oh boy had she wanted to *come* to him.

Was that it? Had the wizard wrapped some sort of lust spell around her? She shook her head. If he'd wrapped any sort of will-sapping spell around her he wouldn't be a wizard. He'd be a warlock. And she'd gotten no sense from him that he was one of *those* spellcasters. They didn't exactly have a shiny happy feel to them.

No, Christopher Beckett was definitely a wizard.

And what was up with the wonder dog routine, anyway? She needed to call Grammy, needed to call her *now*.

She managed to get the irate cat off her lap with only a few minor scratches to add to the ones she'd picked up in the woods. Wrapping the blanket closely around her, she tiptoed farther into the room, looking for a phone.

She was surprised by the look of his home. She'd expected something a little more traditional in décor. Instead, his kitchen had been done in warm light cherry wood with slate floors, surprisingly warm under her bare feet. The countertops and backsplash were warm brown granite that picked up the colors of the slate tile. The stainless steel appliances and fixtures added a modern touch. The smaller appliances had all been cobalt blue; the walls were warm gold, almost the exact shade of Christopher's eyes.

And the great room? He'd brought that gold color in on the contemporary armchairs that flanked his pale cream sofa. The cobalt blue she'd seen in the kitchen was on the walls, the color framing an incredible stainless steel and glass tile fireplace. The floors were a darker shade of cherry than the kitchen cabinets, the wooden coffee table and end tables lighter. She liked it. It was vibrant and warm, like the man himself.

Gah. She had to get out of here before she actually started liking *him*.

She found the phone on one of the end tables, not far from where they'd been sitting on the floor. She dialed the number, knowing Grammy would somehow be expecting her call. Grammy could be a little weird that way. She always seemed to know when one of her grandchildren needed her.

She wasn't wrong. "Hello, Alannah."

She couldn't help but smile. "Hi, Grammy. Do you know

anything about a wizard family named Beckett?" Grammy's gasp was answer enough. The smile fled from Lana's face. "Am I in danger?"

"No! Don't...don't leave. You're safe where you are."

Lana pulled the phone away from her ear and studied it. *Huh. Grammy sounds almost excited.* "Grams. He's a *wizard.*"

"Sweetheart, trust me. *No one* will protect you better than...what did you say his name was?"

"Christopher."

"Christopher Beckett."

"Yes. Gram, somehow I knew his name. How could I know his name?"

"I knew this day would come, just not exactly when. You see, you answered the call."

"What call?"

"He's coming back. Hang up the phone and settle down. Call me in the morning." And Grammy hung up, leaving Lana more confused than ever.

Lana hung up the phone and settled down in front of the fireplace, her mind reeling. Why was Christopher Beckett so much more trustworthy than any other wizard? And why had Grammy sounded happy that she'd fallen into wizard hands?

No. Not wizard hands. *Beckett* hands.

She watched him stroll into the room, two mugs cradled in his hands, and damn near whimpered. She'd never thought a man's walk could be an act of seduction before. Christopher's seemed designed to remind her of what lay under those jeans.

Like she needed reminding. The sight was forever burned into her retinas. She had the feeling her last words on this earth would be something along the lines of "Ooh, naked."

"Here you are." He handed her a mug before settling down

right next to her.

Sneaky dog. "Thank you." She took a sip and nearly orgasmed on the spot. "Holy mama."

His smile was smug. "Good?"

"What did you put in here, liquid sex?"

He sputtered, hot chocolate spraying all over his hands.

She pounded on his back, trying to ease him through the coughing fit. "Sorry."

"No, it's all right. It was just the image of how I would accomplish that." He shook his head, picking up his discarded towel and beginning the process of cleaning up the spilled chocolate. "You have to be one of the most unusual females I've ever met."

"Yeah, well, I'm not the one who howls at the full moon, buster." She put the mug down and hugged the blanket closer around her body. "Speaking of which, you were going to explain it to me?"

He finished wiping his hands off on the towel. "Yes, I was."

She waved her hand at him. "So? Spill." *Give me a reason to trust you other than Grammy.*

"I think we've had enough spills tonight."

"Har har. Funny man."

He sighed. "Long ago, Andrew Beckett, my ancestor, managed to piss off a witch."

Uh-oh.

"The long story short? He'd agreed to marry her, then changed his mind when another, more 'suitable' woman appeared." The way his fingers made little air quotations was kind of cute. "The witch, angry over being jilted, cursed the entire Beckett family."

"Why?" His story sounded sort of familiar. Where had she heard it before?

"Who knows why witches do anything? She chose to curse the entire line, and to this day, Becketts turn into the wolf."

"It doesn't seem like much of a curse to me." She took another sip of chocolate.

"Andrew ate his bride six months after she gave birth to their son."

She made a disgusted face. "Ew."

"His son, knowing what had happened, tried to break the curse."

"And?"

Christopher shuddered. "Let's just say we're lucky he procreated first since the counter–spell, instead of tearing the wolf from him, sort of tore his insides from his outsides."

"Double ew."

"*His* son was determined to find a way to live with the beast. He discovered that, under the right circumstances, he could control the change. Gradually, with each generation, the curse became something different until we could live together with the wolf in peace."

"So the curse became a blessing."

"But not without a price."

"What kind of price?" She yawned, the warmth of the fire and the decadence of the chocolate lulling her. Even the storm, so loud an hour ago, had subsided to a pounding rain, soothing her senses.

He took the mug from her hand. "Sleep. Perhaps in the morning you'll be ready to hear the remainder of the story."

Sleep sounds...good...

Christopher caught her before her head hit the carpet. A simple sleeping draught mixed with the late hour and the strain she'd been under had done its work. It would be morning before she could leave his side. He just hoped whoever she called was willing to leave her in his care.

He couldn't let her go. Not yet. Not until he'd made her his. Definitely not before he'd dealt with the threat Cole represented. He barely knew her and already he would sacrifice his own life to keep her safe. She would learn that she could trust him with her very soul.

He picked her up, marveling at the warm weight of the woman in his arms. The scent of apples was now mixed enticingly with the scent of the chocolate, calling to him, seducing him more thoroughly than he'd ever been seduced by the practiced wiles of other women.

He carried her up the stairs, laying her in his bed, careful not to wake her. The last thing he wanted was her fear. He covered her with the blanket, kissing her forehead before heading out of the room and downstairs to where she'd left her wet clothing. He picked up her jeans, poncho and shirt, planning on washing them for her. She'd need something to wear in the morning.

And that reminded him. He went upstairs again and stripped the still wet underwear from her body, glad for the darkness. He wasn't ready yet to see her completely bared for him in full light, or even pale moonlight. He wasn't certain he'd be able to stop himself from taking her if he did. He carried them downstairs and threw them in the wash with the rest of her clothes. He leaned against the washing machine and hoped he'd done the right thing. She'd been shaking with more than cold; what he'd thought might be arousal was actually fatigue.

She needed rest after her scare in the woods, and he was determined she was going to get it.

He got her purse from by the glass door and carried it into the great room. Opening it he dug out her wallet, determined to know the name of the woman fate had decreed should be his.

Alannah Evans.

The name shot through him with the force of an electrical shock.

It couldn't be. It *shouldn't* be.

But there it was in black and white. Evans. Everything she'd said about wizards suddenly clicked into place.

He picked up the phone and dialed.

"'Lo?"

The sleepy voice on the other end reminded him how late it was, but this was too important to let go. He had to know if he was right. "Gareth?"

"Do you know what fucking time it is, fucktard?"

Christopher sighed. "Alannah Evans."

There was silence for a moment. "What about Alannah Evans?"

The wary caution in Gareth Beckett's now very awake voice was enough to drive Christopher to his feet. "I need to know if she's a member of *the* Evans family."

"Give me a sec." He could hear sheets rustling, knew his brother was climbing out of bed. "Right. According to The Registry, Evans…where's she from?"

He checked her driver's license. "Philadelphia, Pennsylvania."

There was the sound of rustling pages, then the creak of an office chair. "Dude. The Evans family practically *rules*

Philadelphia."

Christopher groaned. "Wonderful."

"Hey, at least she's not a warlock."

"Right. I need a mate who distrusts my kind, not a mate who tries to feed me to demons."

There was a pregnant pause. "Did you say mate?"

Christopher gritted his teeth, cursing himself silently for the slip of his tongue. "Yes."

"A witch."

"Gareth."

"You? *You* mated a *witch?*"

Christopher hung up the phone. Gareth could laugh his ass off all by himself, thank you very much.

Chapter Four

Christopher woke to the feel of a rough tongue on his cheek. He opened one bleary eye to find Alasdair staring at him and purring.

He lifted his head and peered around. His workshop. He'd fallen asleep in his workshop. It wasn't the first time he'd done that, and he doubted it would be the last. He looked down at the book spread out below him, *The Registry of Wizards, Witches and Warlocks*, and groaned.

Alannah *Evans*. A witch, not a wizard.

Well. That will teach me to be careful about how I phrase my summoning spells.

He'd rechecked the runes, the copy of the paper he'd burned that night a month ago, and slowly realized his error. He hadn't specified a *wizard* mate, just one of an older lineage, someone who was born from power, with magic to complement his own.

Apparently the Lord and Lady had seen fit to send him a witch.

Joy. He was never going to hear the end of this. His family would have a field day.

And it was beyond too late now to change it, even if he wanted to. His wolf was completely delighted with the woman upstairs currently curled up in their den, leaving her scent on his sheets and pillows. He wanted to go up there and wallow in her scent, have it wash over him until he couldn't tell where he ended and she began.

And that was only the beginning. He wanted to lick every inch of her body until all he could taste, would ever taste, was her. He longed to thrust inside her, pulling climax after climax out of her until they were both limp and sated, then do all of it all over again.

He buried his head in his hands and groaned. *Now what do I do?* Witches and wizards tended to avoid each other, and with good reason. The precise way wizards performed magic was the antithesis of the breezy way witches performed the same tasks. The hours a wizard spent carefully crafting spells would drive any self-respecting witch insane. The way witches tended to pick up seemingly random objects and blithely cast a spell that garnered the same results drove wizards nuts. Add in the resentment witches felt about how wizards could do things they couldn't do, and the contempt some wizards openly showed toward witches, and you had one hell of a mess destined to give one tired, grumpy wizard a serious migraine.

And the sad part was, just speaking to her last night had shown him he had no choice. Even if he could reverse the summoning, demand a redo from the Gods, he wouldn't. She was just so...beautiful to him. It wasn't her shoulder length, dark brown hair. It wasn't those wide, chocolate brown eyes, her strong jaw, her full lips, or the way she barely came to his chin, causing every protective instinct he had to go on high alert.

No, it was the glimpses of *her* he'd seen last night that sealed his fate. Funny, smart, warily cautious but following him anyway, she'd been brave, strong, resilient.

His.

He'd have to woo his reluctant little witch. He smiled, remembering her reaction to him last night. If he had any doubts about whether or not he could succeed, remembering the quickly banked hunger in her face removed them.

He'd have to deal once and for all with Cole. If Cole tried to lay a hand on Alannah again Christopher wouldn't be able to keep from killing the son of a bitch.

Standing with a sigh, he headed to the kitchen, hoping a nice warm breakfast and some hot coffee would earn him a nice warm reception from the woman in his bedroom.

Lana picked up the phone next to the bed and dialed. "Hey, Grammy."

"Well?"

Lana frowned. She pulled the aqua colored sheet farther up her body and wondered yet again when her underwear had disappeared. *Tricky dog.* "Well what?"

"Did you do the dirty?"

"Grammy!"

"Well, sweetheart, I looked him up in The Registry. I must say, he's...exquisite. And a Beckett, a very powerful family." Grammy paused. "Are you saying you told him no?"

She doesn't have to make it sound like I'd be insane not to do the horizontal bunny hop with the man. "I didn't get the chance." Lana slapped her hand over her mouth, horrified. "I mean, we talked. Just talked."

"Well, look him up, dear. I think you'll be surprised."

"Grammy, something odd, is going on."

"Odd how, dear?"

"He turns into a dog. A wolf, actually."

"Of course he does. He's a Beckett."

Lana gritted her teeth. "You told me shapeshifters were a myth."

"No, I didn't. I told you *natural* shapeshifters are a myth. *Cursed* shapeshifters actually exist."

Lana resisted the urge to bang her head against the wooden headboard until the pain of this conversation stopped. "There's a difference?"

"Worlds of difference, sweetheart."

"Oh. Of course." She remembered what he'd told her the night before. "What happened to the witch who cursed them?"

Grammy was silent for a moment. "Have you ever heard of Theresa Langhorn?"

"Theresa Langhorn? Isn't she the one who—?"

"Yes."

Lana shuddered. *Damn. Just, damn.* "I'd say she paid."

"Threefold, dear. Threefold."

The threefold rule was simple. Whatsoever you sent out into the world would return to you threefold. It was the one major check on the power of a witch or wizard that whatever you did would be done to you in triplicate. If you sent out love, peace and happiness, that would return to you. But if you sent out hatred, pain and degradation...

No one was quite sure how warlocks got around that little impediment, and no true witch or wizard was willing to find out. Grammy liked to say they were probably on a deferred payment plan.

But every now and then a witch lost her temper enough, or a wizard became enraged enough, to show the rest of the magical community *why* they followed the threefold rule.

43

Theresa Langhorn was a perfect, shining example. "Does she still have people in to comb the fur between her toes?"

"Now, dear, we don't speak ill of the stupid."

Lana grinned.

"One last thing before your young man brings you breakfast."

He's making me breakfast? A small part of Lana's heart warmed toward him. It would have been bigger, but just then the sheet slipped, reminding her of her underwear-less state. *Tricky dog.* "What's that, Grammy?"

"Trust your instincts."

"Want to be a great-grandma that badly, huh?" Lana slapped her hand over her mouth again. *What the hell is wrong with me?* She never, *ever* hopped into bed with strange men, let alone strange wolf-man wizard hybrids!

Okay, so, she was kind of already *in* the bed, but that was all his fault. So was her nakedness. And she had no idea where the bathroom was.

That was his fault too.

She ignored her grandmother's laughter, listening for the sound of Christopher's footfalls on the stairs. "I think he's coming."

"Not yet he isn't."

"Grammy!"

"Good-bye, sweetheart. Oh, and remember, he'll protect you no matter what."

"No matter *what* what?"

But Grammy didn't answer. She'd already hung up the phone.

"And the award for most cryptic comment goes to Annabelle

Evans." Lana hung up the phone and wondered which door lead to the bathroom. There were three of them in this ultra-modern, masculine bedroom. The only feminine detail she could see was the cherry stained bed was a four-poster, with rails up top for soft gauzy curtains that weren't there. The comforter was a dark teal, the sheets aqua. The walls were a darker gold than the kitchen, warming up the room.

She had to assume the door across from the bed was the door leading out of the room. One of the others had to lead to the bathroom.

God, she *hoped* one of them led to the bathroom. She felt like she was about to explode.

"Bathroom!"

Christopher plastered himself up against the wall just in time. The naked nymph rushed by him, slamming the door shut behind her.

"Fuck. By the way, nice suit. Is it Armani?"

He manfully swallowed his laugh. "Yes, it is and it is. The master bath is through the other door."

"Thanks!"

She opened the door and streaked past him, the jacket of his suit wrapped around her. He turned, sighing in disappointment when she slammed into the correct room. He almost choked on the laugh at her groan of relief.

When she stepped back into the bedroom, he had himself under control. "Feeling better?" He turned, stopping when he caught sight of her. The charcoal gray jacket hung on her, covering her from neck to mid-thigh, the vee of the jacket revealing the tempting swell of her breasts. "Good morning."

She bit her lip. "Good morning." One of her delicate toes

dug into his carpet. "Where are my clothes?"

"Clothes?" The way she was digging her toe in the carpet had her knee pushing back and forth, back and forth, swinging open the bottom edge of the jacket ever so slightly. Christopher could feel the saliva pooling in his mouth, the bare glimpse of thigh she kept giving him mesmerizing. If she didn't stop soon, his cock was going to burst right out of his jeans.

"The things you put on your body when you aren't wearing your fur?"

"Fur?" He could cover her in fur. He could see them now, naked, skin to skin, writhing on those furs while he took her over and over again.

She looked down at what he was staring at and squeaked. Her toe stopped digging into the carpet. *Damn it.* "Christopher!"

"Hmm?" He dragged his gaze up to her face once more. The amused exasperation there reassured him. He hadn't frightened her with his lust.

Good.

"My clothes. Where are they?"

"They're in the dryer."

"May I have them please?"

No. "I'll bring them up shortly." He waved toward the table by the window. "Breakfast?"

She eyed the table warily. "No woo-woo stuff in the coffee this morning?"

He didn't allow his shock to show in his face. "Woo-woo stuff?"

She approached the table. "You put something in the chocolate last night, didn't you?" Apparently he didn't hide his wince well enough. She sat with a sigh. "You know if my Grammy hadn't told me to trust my instincts you'd be in serious shit right now."

Thank you, Grandmother Evans. He'd have to write the woman an appropriate thank you note. Possibly after the wedding. "What are your instincts telling you?"

She studied him for a moment before picking up her coffee cup. "To trust you. Why, I have no clue, considering you drugged me last night."

He sat across from her, loving the look of his jacket on her skin. He'd think of her now every time he wore the suit. "You can, you know. Trust me, I mean. And you needed some sleep last night. I was worried the flight through the woods would keep you awake all night."

"Uh-huh." Her skeptical look spoke volumes, but apparently she was willing to let it slide. "What exactly is going on, anyway?"

He thought about lying to her for exactly two seconds. He had one shot at this. There was no way he was going to fuck it up. And something told him lying to her was not a good way to get his little witch to trust him. "Do you remember how I told you there was a price to pay for learning to live with the wolf?"

"Yes." She took a bite of her eggs, sighing softly. "Mmm. You're a very good cook, by the way."

He actually blushed. That was the first time a woman had ever complimented him on his cooking. It meant more to him than any compliment he'd ever received before, mostly because she was the one who gave it.

She smiled softly. "Go on."

He cleared his throat. He had the feeling he'd just handed her something he'd miss like hell one day. "Yes. Well, the price for learning to live with the wolf was taking mates."

"Mates."

He nodded.

"You mean more than one?"

"No!" *Lord, don't let her think that. I'm going to be in enough trouble from stuff I do, let alone stuff I don't.* "I meant each Beckett in every generation casts a spell that pulls their perfect mate to them. We never know what fate is going to send us." He kissed her knuckles, enjoying the soft flush creeping up her cheeks. "Fate sent me you."

She put her fork down. "You're essentially werewolves."

He shrugged. He'd heard worse terms. "I suppose. It was the compromise the human made with the wolf. One mate, one *forever* mate who pleases us both."

"Forever mate?"

He nodded. "Wolves mate for life."

He loved watching the emotions crossing her face in rapid succession. "Me?"

He grinned, knowing she'd see the hunger in it. The possession. Hell, the pride. She was taking this a great deal better than some of the Beckett women had.

Right up until she shrieked, that was. "No way!" She leapt from the table. "No fucking way!"

He crossed his arms over his chest, refusing to allow hurt to seep in. She barely knew him. She was entitled to a little rant. Still, what was wrong with him? "Why not?"

"You're a wizard!"

He blinked. So what? "I'm also a werewolf."

She waved it away like it was nothing. "I'm a witch!"

"And?"

"Witches and wizards *don't marry!*"

"Mate."

She glared at him. "We'd kill each other inside of a week, and you know it."

"No, I don't." He was beginning to enjoy the sight of her pacing, waving her arms, the ends of the suit jacket flapping at the tips of her fingers. Each stride revealed a lovely length of leg that had him practically drooling.

"You're too rigid."

"Damn straight." He was becoming so rigid it was beginning to be uncomfortable.

"I'm...what did you say?"

"Hmm? Oh. Nothing. Continue, please."

"You'll think I'm too flighty."

"Mm-hmm."

She waved her arms, the bottom of the jacket hitting the very tops of her thighs. His knees wobbled when a slight glimpse of her pussy teased him before her arms lowered. "The first time I cast a spell you'd feel the urge to correct me."

"And the first time you saw me turn into a wolf?" He nearly fell out of his chair when she made a rude sound. "That...doesn't bother you?"

She looked confused. "Why would it?"

"Why would...? Woman, do you have any idea how many potential partners have turned me down when they hear my last name?" Christopher stalked closer to her, aware he sounded enraged. In some ways he was. The defining characteristic of his family, the one he had always thought would be a sticking point for any potential bride, and she dismissed it like it was *nothing,* harping instead on the fact he was a wizard?

Her low mutter almost got lost in his low growl. "Oh, sure, throw your conquests in my face."

He cupped a hand to his ear. "Care to repeat that?"

She snarled at him. "Look, Captain Oblivious. Witch. Wizard. Oil. Water."

"Werewolf." He cupped her chin, enjoying the way her eyes went wide. "Tasty morsel." He leaned down and licked her neck. He damn near groaned. She tasted incredible.

"I'm not entirely certain I'm on the menu yet."

He smiled against her neck. "You said yet."

"Tricky dog," she grumbled.

He laughed, pulling her into his arms. He lifted his head to stare down into her sulky face. "How about a trial run?"

"You don't even know my name."

"Alannah Evans."

She smacked him in the arm. Hard.

"Ow!"

"How do you know? Your spell?"

Well, maybe one little lie wouldn't hurt. "Yes."

"Uh-huh." Her eyes narrowed. "Where's my purse?"

Busted. "In the great room."

"And did it just happen to fall open at some point in the last twelve hours?"

"Possibly." He made sure he had a good hold of her waist and prepared to throw his thigh in the way of any wandering knees.

When she growled at him, he had to laugh. She sounded so fiercely cute. Not that he'd tell her so. He was a smart man, and enjoyed living with both his balls intact.

"Alannah, I just wanted to know your name."

"Congratulations, now you know. Give me my clothes."

He sighed. "I didn't get to finish my story last night. Would you like to hear it over breakfast?"

"*With* my clothes?"

He rolled his eyes. "All right. I'll return with them shortly." He walked to the door of the bedroom. "Don't go anywhere."

"You really enjoy ordering me to stay, don't you?" He snorted, amused. She crossed her arms, the long ends of his suit jacket flapping over her arms, the edge of the jacket creeping up her thighs. "Besides, unlike some people I know, running around naked in the woods is *not* my idea of a good time."

He allowed a slow smile to cross his face at the thought of her running naked through *his* forest. His gaze ate her up from top to bottom, remembering the look of her dashing through his bedroom. "That's too bad."

Her face was flushed, her expression a mixture of embarrassment and heat. "Clothes, perv!"

He laughed softly and walked out of the bedroom, ignoring her mutters. He returned swiftly with her clothes, hoping to catch one more glimpse of creamy thigh. He'd taken the time last night to make sure her outfit was clean and dry, knowing she'd more than likely want her clothes. He, on the other hand, would be more than happy to keep her naked for the rest of her life.

He handed her clothes to her with a small bow. "Here you are, m'lady."

She took them, smiling warily. "Thanks." She gestured toward the bathroom. "I'll be right back." She headed for the bathroom, giving him an unreadable look before closing the door behind her.

Christopher settled into one of the chairs by the small table, filling his plate with food. She might not be hungry, but

51

he was starving.

She came out a few minutes later dressed in everything but the poncho, socks and boots she'd been wearing the night before. "Thank you for washing my clothes."

He smiled, trying to look harmless. "You're welcome." He stood and held out her chair. "Are you ready to finish breakfast?"

She studied him intently for a moment, the scrutiny making him vaguely uneasy, before settling daintily into the chair. "Thank you." She took another bite of the cooling eggs, then a sip of the coffee. "Mmm. It's good, even cold." She smiled at him. "Now. Forever mates. Ancestral curses. A daily yearning for Kibbles 'n Bits."

Christopher winced. "Hmm. Yes, where were we?"

"Let's start with what makes you think I'm your mate and go from there." She took a bite of crisp bacon, her eyes closing in pure pleasure. "Damn. Okay, for bacon this good you get to call me Lana."

He swallowed hard. He wanted to see that look on her face while he fucked her into the mattress.

Her eyes opened and something of what he was feeling must have shown in his face because she retreated from him, wiping the pleasure away with a quick shake of her head.

Christopher took a sip of his coffee, trying to ignore the way his hand trembled. He'd never wanted anyone so badly in his entire life. What made it worse was his wolf pushing him to pounce and mate. He was having a hard time resisting both his own instincts and his wolf's. "About a month ago I cast a spell."

"A love spell?" She was frowning at him now, her eyes turning hard.

He glared back. "Do I look like I want the universe to slap

me upside the head?" Her expression eased. "Wizards follow the threefold rule as well, you know." And one of the worst spells to cast was one forcing someone to do or be something they weren't. The Lord and Lady took a dim view to that sort of thing.

She had the grace to look sheepish. "Sorry."

"The spell is one my ancestor came up with after several years of research. Each Beckett male, when...certain feelings become overwhelming, gather the ingredients, place the Beckett ring in the circle, and cast the spell."

"The Beckett ring?"

"It's the ring my great-grandfather used in the spell to call his mate to him. It became my great-grandmother's engagement ring." He liked the soft smile curving her lips. "When his brother was ready, the ring was lent to him, the spell cast, and his mate came to him within a month."

She frowned thoughtfully. "So every Beckett male casts this spell and boom! Instant girlfriend?"

"More like instant fiancée."

Her expression turned from intrigued to mildly panicked within seconds. "Uh..."

He placed his hand over hers, reveling in the feel of her smooth skin. "Don't worry, we'll keep the engagement short." He kissed her fingers, resisting the urge to taste her skin again. He already knew she would be addictive.

"And you think it was the spell that brought me here?"

"I'm certain of it." He sat back, sipping from his coffee. Her face was so expressive. Every emotion she felt flitted across it. He was certain she'd never be able to tell him a lie without his knowing it.

"Well, bud, let me set you straight. It turns out I was there for a bachelorette party, with male strippers and everything, and if my car hadn't broken down on the road, you'd never have met me."

She smirked at him with an air of triumph, oblivious to the fact that his coffee mug had begun to crack. *Male strippers? She'd been around half-naked men last night?* He had the urge to shred the bright turquoise V-neck T-shirt she was wearing, knowing where she'd been the night before. It read *Go Forth and Sin Some More.* He'd smiled when he'd seen it last night, but now? Now it needed to meet a trashcan. He set the mug down carefully on his empty plate, hoping she wouldn't notice the slowly spreading coffee under the mug. "And what drove you into the woods, Lana? Lust?"

She opened her mouth, the closed it, looking startled. "Instinct."

"Instinct." Interesting. "And what kept you from accepting Cole's offer of help?"

She frowned again. "Was that his name?"

"Mm-hmm."

"He was a wizard." She waved her hands vaguely. "And his aura was funky."

He bit his lip to keep from smiling. "Funky?"

"Yuk it up, furball, but you didn't see the colors swirling around him. Black and icky green. Not the good green like grass, but the glowing eerie shit that scares you in bad horror movies."

"Furball?" *Wait.* "How did you know he was a wizard?"

She shrugged. "The same way I knew you were a wizard. It's in your magic."

He blinked. "I had no idea you were a witch."

"Really?" The surprise in her voice turned into a smug

smile. "Cool."

He rolled his eyes. "I can show you the spell I cast to call you to me if you like."

She tilted her head. "You think I'll understand your spell?"

"I don't see why not."

Her mouth opened again but nothing came out, the surprise there nearly causing him to laugh. She must not have expected him to offer to show her the spell. "Huh. I never thought I'd see the day a wizard offered to show a witch his workroom." She stood. "Bring it on."

He grinned. "Follow me."

"Where have I heard that before?" She followed him out of the bedroom and down the stairs. "Oh, wait, I remember now. I think it was the time just before you drugged my hot chocolate."

"Can you *prove* I drugged your hot chocolate?"

She growled, then huffed out a breath. "No."

"Well then." He opened the door to his workroom. "Here you are."

She walked past him into the room only his family was allowed into. His wards let her in easily, barely rippling around her. "Whoa." She put her hand to her forehead. "What was *that*?"

"My protection spells."

Her eyes went wide, her face paling. "Am I about to experience being inside out?"

He huffed out a startled laugh. "No, of course not!"

She turned to look up at him, her gaze following him when he moved into the workroom. "Because you're with me, right?"

He merely raised one brow.

"Right?"

He sat behind his desk, ignoring the open Registry. He had no doubt she would look him up in it soon enough, the same way he'd looked her up. "It let you through because it knows you're family."

She sat in front of his desk with a thump. "Oh."

He leaned forward. "Welcome home."

Chapter Five

Welcome home? Oh crap. What have I gotten myself into this time? Lana stared at the wizard behind the desk, trying to ignore how the mambo-dancing butterflies came back every time she saw him. "My home is in Philadelphia."

"Is it?"

"Geez, I can't wait until you and Grammy meet. The entire conversation will be questions and obscure Confucius-type conversations."

The slow, sultry smile was taking over his mouth again, causing the butterflies to go from mambo to Macarena in two seconds flat. "Do you want to see the spell?"

"Uh-huh." She cleared her throat, wondering if he'd heard how breathless her answer had been. "Yes, I would."

He pointed to a table on the other side of the room. "Help yourself."

She stood, walking toward the table covered in rose-colored cloth. She stared down at the runes, the remainders of the cinnamon incense still scenting the air. Burnt scraps of blue—*Blue? Why blue?*—paper lay in the bottom of the cold cauldron, left there until the spell was complete. Colored candles were placed strategically, almost but not quite making sense to her. A rose and an iris, stems braided through an emerald ring, lay across a golden plate, their petals undimmed by the passage of time. And two special candles, one carved with the symbol for male, one with the symbol of female, touched, their wax pooled together, delicately binding them together. "Whoa."

Chris's finger reached out and stroked the female candle. Lana could swear she felt his touch through her whole body. "When the candles finally touched one another I knew you were near." The husky whisper sent a shiver down her spine. His hand reached out and took hers, gently cradling it. Lana watched, fascinated, as he took her fingers and stroked the male candle. She felt him quiver behind her. "I could almost feel your presence." His breath stirred her hair; his nearness warmed her in places she hadn't realized had been cold. His free arm snaked around her waist, pulling her gently against him. She could feel his erection pressing against the small of her back. "I could almost taste how sweet you would be." A soft kiss pressed through her hair to reach the side of her neck. "If Cole had laid one hand on you, he'd be dead."

She shivered at the sudden coldness in his voice. "I can take care of myself."

She felt his smile against her skin. "I know. I was there, remember?"

She licked her lips, ignoring the way his mouth was tickling her skin. "So you still think I'm the one the spell called?"

"Mm-hmm." He nibbled, sharp teeth gently scraping against her. "I know you are."

She lifted her shoulder, dislodging that distracting, totally tempting mouth. "How do you know?"

He shifted their joined hands and touched the emerald ring.

Warmth flowed up her arm, twining around them both like a sleek silken rope. Her magic flared inside her, meeting and answering the call of the spell, allowing it to settle inside her.

58

She felt the brush of his cock against her ass and moaned.

His quickly indrawn breath let her know he felt the spell settle into place, joining them with invisible bonds. "I know." He turned her, pulling her against him, cradling her between his legs and lifting her onto the worktable. "And so do you."

"Chris—"

She didn't get anything else out. His mouth descended onto hers in a ravishing kiss. One broad hand buried itself in her hair, holding her head right where he wanted it. He fucked her mouth with his tongue, owning it in a way no other man ever had. The other cradled her hip, pulling her to the edge of the table, enabling him to thrust his jean-clad erection against her throbbing pussy.

Power, seduction, heat, all poured off of him, settling into her with incredible force. She'd never felt such craving for another person before. She trembled with it. Without thought her legs splayed wide to accommodate his hips. Reaching out to steady herself, her fingers brushed against the emerald ring. Desire flooded through her, hot and wet and throbbing.

She tried to take control of the kiss, her only thought to satisfy the pure *want* coursing through her. She could feel her nipples beading painfully under her bra.

"Fuck, *need* you." Chris nipped his way down her throat. He thrust against her, his hardness taunting her under the barrier of their jeans. He reached desperately for the hem of her shirt, and fuck if she didn't help, grabbing the edge and ripping it over her head, exposing her white cotton bra. With a groan he bent to her, taking her into his mouth, sucking her nipples one at a time until she was groaning and thrusting up against him.

He matched her move for move, mock-fucking her against the table, never letting her nipples out of his mouth. The sensation was incredible, intense beyond belief. She clenched her hands, her body tense with anticipation. She was so damn close to orgasm she wanted to scream. She barely registered the round hard object in her hand. "Fuck me, please God, fuck me."

With a growl he pulled free. His expression was wild, his eyes, those incredible golden eyes nearly swallowed by the pupils. He yanked desperately at her jeans, tugging them down her legs, pausing half way down to lick her pussy through her cotton panties. "So good." He shoved the panties aside and rasped his tongue against her clit. "You taste so fucking good."

He ate her out, licking and sucking her into his mouth until she was fucking his face, desperate to come. She reached toward him and grabbed his head, holding him steady. The pressure built and built until she arched into his mouth with a cry that barely sounded human.

Her panties and jeans hit the floor before she'd completely come down from one of the most intense orgasms she'd ever experienced. Her eyes were still crossed when he yanked down his zipper and pulled out an impressive cock, stroking it once or twice before sinking into her still quivering pussy.

"Mine."

He grabbed her hips, slowly pulling out of her. Then he slowly sank back in, taking his time fucking her. He was watching his cock slide into her, and she couldn't help but look too.

It was incredible, watching him fuck her. He pulled her to him, closer to the edge of the table, his hands clenching on her hips. Bending down he took her nipple into his mouth and sucked just hard enough to have her moaning.

"Chris."

"Hmm?"

"God, Chris, faster. Harder."

She felt his smile against her breast. "Faster and harder." He lifted up from her, his cock poised just inside her, the flared head barely brushing a spot that had her body screaming hallelujah. "Are you sure?"

She was so close to coming she could scream. She grabbed the back of his neck and pulled until they were nose to nose. "Fuck me now or you *will* regret it."

His grin was filled with male satisfaction. "Yes, ma'am."

He began stroking into her so hard she swore she could feel him nudging the back of her throat. *Oh shit.* She was going to be bruised inside and out. She'd *never* been fucked so hard or so well. How did he know just where to touch her, to push her? It bordered on just this side of painful, but damn if she couldn't feel her whole body clenching around him. She was moaning, caught in the dance of their bodies, watching his face clench while he fucked her. Their eyes stayed glued to each other, neither one giving an inch while he pounded into her.

"Come for me, little witch."

She gritted her teeth against the building pleasure. "You first, wolfman."

She automatically wrapped her legs around his hips when his hands left her. They didn't stay gone long, however. The fingers of one hand plucked at her nipples, sending shards of exquisite pain straight to her clit. When the other hand reached down to do the same thing to her clit she damn near lost it, bucking up against him so hard she almost threw him off of her.

She was close, so damn close, but fuck if she was going alone.

She glared up at him in challenge and clenched her inner muscles with every ounce of will she had. He brushed her clit in just the right damn spot to have her seeing stars.

Lana screamed, her back bowing until her head rested on the table, her entire body pulsing around him. He howled, pouring himself into her in agonized bliss.

He collapsed on top of her with a groan, gasping against her neck. She could feel him still twitching inside her.

He kissed the side of her neck gently. "Mine."

Lana's eyes popped open. *Oh fuck. What have I done?*

He bent, taking her mouth sweetly, gently, before letting her go with a sigh. "I think you killed me. I'm dead and in Nirvana."

She couldn't help it. She giggled before she could stop herself.

"Oh sure. Laugh at the dead man."

"Trust me, you're not dead."

She could feel his grin tickling the side of her neck. Part of her loved the sensation. Another part was seriously freaked out she'd let this happen at all.

"How do you know?"

She clenched her muscles, secretly pleased when he swallowed. "I can feel your, um, *pulse.*"

His shoulders shook. He pushed up against her, his softening cock squishing slightly. "Mm. I like it when you take my pulse, Nurse Evans."

"I bet." She pushed on his shoulders. "Get up, wolfman."

He practically purred against her shoulder. "*Your* wolfman." He stood up lazily, his cock slipping from her dripping pussy. He stretched, his shirt pulling tight against his chest.

Damn, we didn't even get completely naked. "That's still debatable."

He paused in pulling up his jeans. "It is?"

She sat up, wincing at the tender feeling in her pussy. She was going to feel his fucking for a day or two. "One incredible orgasm does not eternal mates make."

"*Two* incredible orgasms."

She waved her hand, trying for nonchalance. The trembling in her hand showed how miserably she failed. "Fine, two."

He watched her gather her clothes and get dressed again, his frown turning into a scowl. "You accepted me."

"I fucked you. There's a difference." She crossed her arms over her chest and glared right back at him, trying to ignore the blush stealing over her cheeks.

His gaze darted to her neck and, with a wince, his expression relaxed into something akin to...sorrow? "We *are* destined to be together, but you aren't ready to accept it yet." He pulled away, giving her room to breathe. He shook himself all over and visibly relaxed. "All right, Lana. There are other things we need to discuss anyway."

We're ready! We're ready! The butterflies were back in force and wailing up a storm. Lana did her best to ignore them. "Like?"

"Like the fact you'll be staying here until I know exactly what Cole is up to."

Dream on, wolfman. "Pffft. Yeah, right."

He blinked, shocked. "Excuse me?"

"I have a life in Philadelphia, and spell or no spell, I'm not moving in with a man I met last night. Sorry, but if you ordered a wife in twenty minutes or less then you dialed the wrong number."

"He threatened your life."

"Yes, he did. And I know just how to handle it too."

"Oh really?"

"Yes. Really."

He crossed his arms over his chest. "How?"

"Grammy."

His head tilted to the side, just like the wolf's had the night before. "Grammy?"

"Annabelle Evans."

The frown lightened. "Oh. Grammy." He took a deep breath. "Still, I'd prefer it if you remained here."

"I wouldn't." She looked around the workroom. "You have a phone in here?"

"Alannah."

"I need to go home, Chris."

"You *are* home."

"No. I'm in *your* home. I need my people around me, my things, my protections."

"Why?"

Poor guy. He sounds so frustrated. Still, she wasn't about to back down on this one. If he thought he'd get his way every single time, they'd have a horrible time of it.

She tried to ignore the little voice quivering inside her, pointing out how she'd just accepted what he'd been telling her all along. No way was she ready to deal with it yet. "Witches and wizards, remember? I need to know what's being done to defend me."

He had the nerve to look offended. "You'll have me to defend you."

"And since you're a wizard I'll understand very little of what you're doing. Defend me all you like, but I'll be in Philadelphia while you do it."

His eyes narrowed. "Compromise?"

She eyed him warily. "What kind of compromise?"

"You want to go to Philadelphia, where your family can protect you?"

"Yes," she drawled, wondering what the catch was.

"Then Philadelphia it is, where your family will protect you." And he gave her a smug male smile that raised every hair on the back of her neck.

Lana groaned. "Why do I have the feeling I just lost?"

Chapter Six

Christopher shut the hood of Lana's car and smiled. It was truly and sincerely dead. From the looks of it, the funeral was long overdue too. "Sorry, I don't believe I can fix it."

"Damn." She bit the tip of her finger. He gave in to the urge to pull it from her mouth and kiss the small hurt. "Anywhere around here I can have it towed?"

"Leave it. I'll call my brothers and have them deal with it."

She stared at him.

"All right. *You* call my brothers and have them deal with it." He could tell she was still trying to stare him down, but it wasn't working. She wasn't going to get her way all the time, or they'd have an awful relationship. He handed her his cell phone and placed his hand at the small of her back. "Call Gareth. Speed dial three." He began to guide her toward his SUV, the sleek black Equinox looking completely out of place next to her old, battered beige Volkswagen. "He'll make sure your, um, car is taken care of."

She glared at him and dialed the phone. He knew the exact moment when Gareth's voice mail came on. He'd helped his brother record it, after all. "Hello, you've reached Gareth Beckett. If this is important, then you know how to reach me. If it's not important, don't bother leaving a message." *Beep.*

Lana blinked. "Uh, hi. This is Alannah Evans. Um, your

really weird brother has kidnapped me and he wants me to ask you to deal with my broken-down car. I totally understand if you want to call the cops and tell them where I'm at, which right now would be in Christopher's black Equinox heading toward Philadelphia, Pennsylvania license plate number six one five... Damn, it hung up."

He snorted, amused. "I did not kidnap you."

"What would you call it?"

"Giving my fiancée a ride to her grandmother's house." Whether she liked it or not, she was his. The sex in his workroom just confirmed it for him, but until she accepted it, the spell would remain incomplete.

"Will you stop with the fiancée stuff?"

He smiled. "All right...mate."

He laughed, delighted, when she snarled at him. She waved her finger at him. "I still haven't accepted it, you know."

"You will, sweetheart."

She ignored him, turning on the radio and staring out the window.

It was a two-hour drive from his house to Philadelphia, and almost all of it was spent in silence, listening to the radio. It wasn't until they were on the outskirts of the city that she spoke again, giving him quiet directions to a section of the city known locally as South Philly. The brick row houses were well maintained, with wide steps or pretty brick front porches with metal railings. The occasional tree had been planted in perfect holes cut into the pavement, then surrounded by decorative bricks. The neighborhood had a very homey feel to it despite the fact that, not far away, several stadiums had been built for the major league sports teams.

The only problem he had was the old trolley tracks slicking

up the road. He found himself driving more to the left than he was really comfortable with. "Why don't they cover those?"

"Cover what?"

He gestured out the front windshield. "The trolley tracks."

She looked at him like he'd lost his mind. "They're a historical monument. Look up." He did, seeing the wires criss-crossing the road. "Those lines are trolley lines, still intact. These tracks are some of the oldest in the United States. You put a trolley down and it could still run all over Philly. Well, most of Philly." She waved her hand. "No way would we cover those up."

"Oh. So you have a trolley system like San Francisco?"

"Pfft. No, not like San Francisco. We don't have any trolley cars."

He blinked. "Tracks and lines, but no cars?"

She rolled her eyes. "Politics are a bitch. The cars were supposed to be put into use, but things keep getting in the way." She shrugged and pointed. "Turn left here."

He blinked, confused, but turned anyway.

"Okay, find a place to park."

He looked around. Half the potential spots had a handicapped sign right next to them. The other half were all taken. "You're kidding, right?"

She smirked. "Just keep looking."

He eventually found a spot three blocks from where she'd told him to keep looking. They got out and began walking. "Okay, we're close to Oregon Avenue, which means lots of good food, some decent grocery stores, and access to most of Philly. Front Street leads to I-95, so that's not too far away, and Broad leads to Center City and more shopping, with some theaters and stuff." She crossed the street, vaguely checking for oncoming cars. "You ever been to the Gallery?"

He followed, wrinkling his nose at the smell of exhaust. This was one of the many reasons he'd chosen to leave Pittsburgh behind and move to a more rural area. "Can't say I have."

"Huh. I'll have to take you there."

He kept his smile to himself.

"Anyway, we can order in some cheese steaks tonight, maybe catch a game on TV. You like baseball?"

"Not so much." He was more of a hockey fan, but saying he rooted for the Pittsburgh Penguins might get him dead in this neighborhood.

"Oh. The Phillies are playing in town this week, so we'll see more traffic than usual." She strode up some steps and banged on the door. "Now play nice or I'll put you in the dog house."

"Woof."

She snickered, but before she could reply, the door opened. A small woman with salt and pepper hair stood there in jeans and a T-shirt. Her feet were bare, and a small frilly apron was around her waist. "Alannah?"

"Hi, Grammy. Can we come in?"

Grammy? The five foot tall, barefoot woman was Annabelle Evans, head of one of the most powerful covens on the east coast?

"Of course! And you're Christopher Beckett." Annabelle Evans held out her hand. "Welcome to my home, Mr. Beckett."

He took her hand, shocked at the strength of her grip. "A pleasure, Mrs. Evans." He ignored the tendrils of magic snaking up his arm. He knew she was merely testing his strength and his ability to take care of her granddaughter, and he didn't blame her. He might have done the same thing himself if it was

69

his granddaughter. Besides, if Annabelle Evans wanted him dead, she really didn't need to touch him to do it. She was one of the strongest witches in the United States, and had the council seat to prove it.

He followed Lana into the house, prepared to see a home done in the style of his own grandmother's, somewhat fussy but warm and welcoming. Instead what he found was a remarkably eclectic looking home, with bright colors, modern furniture and homey little touches. The dark hardwood floors were counteracted by the traditional camel-colored sofa. The sofa faced a Spanish-style TV armoire with a TV currently tuned to...

Goddess, was one of the most powerful witches in the land addicted to America's Next Top Model reruns?

A coffee table, the top done in a bright mosaic of tiles, was flanked by two bright, modern turquoise chairs. The camel-colored curtains stood out against the wall color, a lighter turquoise than what was on the chairs. Looking toward the back of the house, he could see through an arch the dining room, done in a much darker turquoise, an ebony-stained Queen Anne dining set taking up most of the space. Over the dining set was a multi-tiered sculptural chandelier made of what looked like Murano glass.

Beyond the dining room was the kitchen, and what little he could see of it told him it was done in the same mix of styles as the rest of the house.

The only indication that a witch lived here was the small shelf on the wall. A plaque bearing a sun and moon melded together in a seamless, yin-yang type portrait held pride of place. It was flanked by two candles, one silver and the other gold. A wooden burner held the ashes of what smelled like jasmine incense. He couldn't tell if she'd done spellwork there recently or simply lit the incense for the joy of it, but it still screamed "altar" to him even without the trappings he'd often seen in books or on his own altar.

He liked it. It fit the woman who stood in front of him, chatting with her granddaughter. What he didn't like was the exasperated tone she was addressing Lana in. "Why didn't you stay at Mr. Beckett's house?"

Lana gaped. "I barely know the man!"

"Didn't I tell you he'd protect you?"

"Yes."

"So?" Annabelle tapped her foot.

Lana shot him a look, like the fact her grandmother appeared annoyed was all his fault. "He says I'm his mate. He cast some sort of spell and says I was the answer or something."

Annabelle nodded. "You *did* answer the call. I already told you so, remember?"

Lana threw her hands up in the air. "Someone threatened to kill me!"

"And Christopher will protect you from him."

Christopher decided to interrupt before things got ugly. Lana was turning suspiciously red in the face, and he didn't think it was all from anger. He'd caught a flash of hurt there, quickly masked. "Excuse me."

"Well, gee, stupid me for thinking my family might help me."

Annabelle sighed. "Christopher has dealt with this person for a long time. The protections he has in place were designed to keep him out. Why do you think I told you to stay?"

Lana frowned. "Wizard versus wizard?"

"Exactly." Annabelle led her granddaughter over to the sofa. "Sit, and I'll finish lunch. Then you can tell me why you think

71

it's necessary to stay here rather than at Christopher's."

"Because something tells me it's the last thing this guy would expect us to do."

Annabelle stopped. Christopher studied Lana's face, seeing for the first time the serene certainty that she was right. "You think it will take him some time to find us?"

She smiled. "Exactly."

Well. Damn. He had an inkling of what she was up to now. "God, I love a smart woman." He ignored her blush. "You're right. I doubt he knows who you are, but it won't take him long to figure it out, and when he does he might target you."

She beamed at him. "Exactly."

"While we stay here and work out the best way to keep you safe, I'll contact my family and see how they can help us figure out what Cole is up to. Deal?"

"Deal."

"At the first sign your grandmother is in danger, I'm taking you back to my house." He held up his hand when she opened her mouth to protest. "I will not put your family in danger. That is non-negotiable."

"If he's keeping an eye on *your* family, he'll become suspicious if they all head over to Philly. How will you handle it?"

He took her hand and began absently playing with her fingers, the motion soothing him. He hadn't really touched her since the incredible lovemaking in his workroom. It felt like it had been longer than a few hours. "I'll have to tell them to mask themselves from scrying. It will buy us a little time, but not much."

"And in the meantime we try and figure out what you did to piss someone off so much they threaten to kill your supposed mate."

He growled. *Supposed* mate? He really needed to work on correcting her stubborn impression he'd gotten the wrong woman.

She patted his head. "Down, Fido."

He took her hand in his and leaned into her. "How can you deny the magic that coursed through you when you touched the ring?" He kept his voice soft so Mrs. Evans wouldn't hear them arguing.

"How would you feel if a complete stranger walked up to you and said, 'Congratulations! You get to spend the rest of your life with me whether you like it or not!'?" Lana was also keeping her voice soft, yet still managed to sound like she was yelling at him.

Goddess, she was so cute when she was pissed. "That's not true."

"Yes, it is."

"You could walk away from me." His heart was pounding. *Please don't walk away from me.*

She raised an eyebrow at him in disbelief. "Really?"

"Yes. You could throw me out and declare you want nothing to do with me. Eventually, if you held strong, I would have to give up and go away."

"And then what?"

He knew what would happen then, but he didn't want to guilt her into staying with him. He wanted her to stay because she wanted to. So he remained silent, ignoring her deepening glare.

Finally she blew her bangs out of her eyes, glaring at him. "You are *so* stubborn."

He couldn't help but laugh. "*I'm* stubborn?" He stroked her cheek. "What is the worst that could happen, Alannah? You fall in love with a man completely devoted to you, who will never cheat on you or leave you. A man willing to lay down his life for you if need be." She had the deer in the headlights look again. He stroked his thumb across her full lips, teasing them both with the promise of a kiss, hoping to soothe her. "Give me a chance. Learn me, get to know me. I may surprise you, despite the fact I'm a wizard."

"A wolf wizard."

He frowned, his heart sinking. Had she lied about it not bothering her? "I thought it didn't bother you."

"It doesn't, not really. But it's a part of you I'll need to get to learn if I'm going to go through with this."

"Do you want to see me change?"

She blinked. "Here?"

"Well, we could take it upstairs..."

She was glaring at him again. "Here's good."

He raised his voice. "Mrs. Evans?"

"You can call me Annabelle, Christopher."

"Thank you. Would you mind staying in the kitchen for about ten minutes?"

Silence. "Only ten?"

"Grammy!" Lana buried her face in her hands but not before he caught sight of her reddening cheeks.

He took pity on her. "Lana wants to meet my wolf." There was a difference between their meeting in the woods and what Lana wanted now. She needed to *meet* the wolf, touch him without the threat of Cole behind them, possibly even bond with him. It would be another rite of passage for both of them.

"Ah." Annabelle's voice was knowing. "Very well then. I'll have another cup of coffee."

"Thank you, Annabelle."

"You're welcome."

He tipped Lana's face up. "Are you ready?"

She nodded.

Christopher stepped away and made sure the windows were covered. Satisfied, he began stripping. He chuckled when Lana turned away. "You've already seen, touched and felt everything, Lana."

"Don't remind me, wolfman."

He stepped out of his pants, fully nude. "You can turn around now." He waited for her to be fully turned before calling his wolf to him.

He hated the word summon. It implied his wolf did his bidding. It was more than that; it was a blending of souls, a partnership where each met the needs of the other. So he called his wolf and invited him in.

His wolf answered. They flowed together, the change overtaking his body, the wolf becoming dominant. He opened his eyes, almost afraid of what Lana's reaction would be.

She fell to her knees in front of him, the wonder on her face easing most of his fears. "You're beautiful."

He tilted his head into her palm, eager for her touch. She stroked him, running her fingers through his fur, scratching behind his ear. He sighed happily and licked her cheek.

"Ew. Dog breath."

He growled playfully, his tail wagging back and forth. He held on to the desire to pounce on her. His wolf wanted to play with their mate.

"Gee, Grandpa, what big teeth you have."

He shook his head and retreated, beginning the change again. He had the urge to run, a need he always had when his

75

wolf was dominant. A need he couldn't indulge in South Philadelphia. And the thought of Lana taking him walkies on a leash?

Hell to the no.

He reached first for his underwear, slipping it back on. "So we're agreed we'll stay here until Cole finds us."

"But in separate bedrooms," she added quickly.

He rolled his eyes and reached for his pants. "Fine. We'll have separate bedrooms."

"Don't sound so grumpy. Next thing you know you'll be whining and giving me puppy dog eyes."

He gave her his best sad-sack face. "Can you resist puppy dog eyes?"

She bit her lip. "I hereby exercise my fifth amendment rights against self incrimination."

He chuckled softly. "I *like* you." He stroked her hair away from her eyes, lingering in its silky sweetness. "Maybe some day soon you'll like me too."

Her expression turned serious. "I hereby exercise my—"

He kissed the rest of the sentence away, forgetting where they were, forgetting everything but the taste, the scent of her.

When his lips left hers she sighed. "I am in *so* much trouble."

Chapter Seven

Grammy had insisted on having Chris call her Annabelle. And he did, striking up a relaxed conversation over ham and cheese sandwiches and barbeque potato chips, sitting in her kitchen at Grammy's comfortable ebony stained banquette. He'd even offered to sit on one of the long benches behind the table, his back to the wall, leaving the chairs for Lana and Grammy. He was calm, polite, a total gentleman.

She wondered what he was up to.

"So it's all right if Lana and I stay here, at least for a little while?"

Grammy was nodding in cheery agreement. "Of course you're both welcome to stay here. Do you have any idea why Cole is so eager to hurt you and Lana?"

Christopher frowned and rubbed at his forehead. "I have no idea. There's some bad blood between us, but nothing that would warrant attacking Lana." He cleared his throat. "Last I heard he was happily ensconced in Pittsburgh along with his family."

Lana watched Chris gulp, his face turning pale. He discreetly pushed his plate away. "I need to do a little research, find out exactly what he thinks I've done this time."

"This time?" Lana watched Chris take a sip of soda, wincing before he put it down. Something wasn't right. He was flushed, then pale, and he was beginning to shake. Every instinct she had sat up and began screeching. She pressed her hand against his forehead. "Chris, you're burning up."

"Too soon to get sick from the rain." He coughed into his napkin, his body wracked with shudders.

"Sorry, wolfman, but it looks like you're wrong." She stood and pulled him from the bench. She staggered, his full weight hitting her, nearly dropping them both to the ground. "Whoa! Steady, Chris."

"Not wrong. We don't get sick like this." He coughed again, his voice hoarse. She winced in sympathy at the wet sound.

"Grammy? Blue room?" At Annabelle's nod, she steered Chris through the kitchen toward the stairs at the front of the house. "Most people would catch cold after being out naked in the rain."

She took hold of the banister, pausing when he grabbed hold of her wrist. "Not like *this*."

She bit her lip, narrowing her eyes at him. "You think this is magical?"

"Yes."

She pulled him up the stairs, one dragging step at a time. She agreed with him, and it scared her. It had come on so *fast*. "You think I did it?"

He looked horrified. "No! Cole."

"Damn. We *really* need to figure out what you did to piss him off." She pushed open the door at the end of the hall, pulling him into the blue bedroom. A twin bed was covered in a deep blue comforter, the walls done a paler blue. It was a quiet, soothing room, perfect for a sick man.

He tried to smile, but she could tell it was too much effort. "Tell me about it."

She pulled the comforter and sheet down before settling him on the bed. "Get some rest."

She jumped when he grabbed her hand again, his worried, fevered gaze holding her own. "Are you sick?"

"I'm fine, Chris. Whatever this is hasn't affected me." The relief on his face melted a little bit more of her resistance to him. How could she stay mad over the mate spell when he obviously cared so much already? She couldn't resist brushing his hair off his forehead. "Don't worry. I'll take care of you." She watched him slip into unconsciousness, more frightened than she could ever remember being.

Lana double-checked the chicken soup she'd made, making sure the magic rose from it properly. If Chris was right, and this Cole person was responsible for his illness, then the soup was only step two.

Step one was already in Chris's room, hopefully absorbing some of the sickness plaguing him. She checked the ginger and anise seed tea on the counter and decided it had steeped long enough.

Grammy broke a cinnamon stick in half and added it to the mixture, nodding slightly. "That should do it." She put the tea on the tray, smiling at Lana.

Lana added the heavily herbed chicken soup and picked up the tray. "I'm going to go ahead and take this up."

Grammy ladled out a bowl of the soup. "Go on, sweetie. I know you're worried about him." She held up her bowl. "I'm just going to have some preventative medicine just in case."

Lana toed open the door to the bedroom, not sure if she'd find him conscious or not.

"Hey."

She smiled when she saw Chris's wan smile. *Good, maybe the first part of the spell is working.* He'd scared her, the way he'd just passed out earlier. "Hey yourself."

She carried the tray over to the bed, waiting until he'd managed to partially prop himself up. "Here you go."

"What's this?"

"Lunch."

He picked up the tea and sniffed. "What's in this?"

"Cinnamon, anise seed and ginger."

He eyed the cup warily. "Really?"

"Drink it."

He eyed her just as warily. "I pissed you off that badly?"

"Chris." Her hands hit her hips, and she stared him down, waiting for him to give in.

He made a face and took a sip. "Mmm. It's actually not too bad."

"Good, then you'll finish it."

"And chicken soup? You spoil me, darling." He took a bite. "It's...um, spicy."

"And spelled, so finish it."

He choked.

"Don't be a wuss. Go ahead and finish it."

He sniffed, sounding stuffed up, but gamely took another bite.

She pulled a chair over to the side of his bed and settled in, curling her legs under her. "Nearest I can figure, if you're right and Cole is behind this, he must have gotten a hair or something off of you during the fight in the woods last night."

He grimaced. "Thought of that after I woke up."

80

"And if he got your hair, he got the hair of the wolf, right?"

"Yes," he drawled.

"So switching to wolf won't cure you like you've been thinking."

He looked shocked. "How did you know I was thinking of shifting?"

She patted his knee. "Just a wild guess."

He looked baffled, but it wasn't something she could explain to him. She just...*knew*. "Anyway, I have the feeling if you shifted to wolf, things would actually get worse, not better."

"Because the spell is tied to the wolf's hair, not mine."

She beamed at him. "Exactly."

"Then shouldn't we be trying to cure the wolf?"

"Most of the remedies in the soup work on canines and humans, so we should be all right." She'd made sure to look up ingredients on the Internet before beginning the soup, just in case she accidentally did more harm than good.

"Oh." He took another sip of tea, much to her delight. "So the chicken soup and tea are the remedies?"

"And the plant."

He eyed the plant on his nightstand. The leaves were beginning to droop. A few had turned brown. "Ah."

"I've taken a clipping. Even if this plant dies it will live on." She fingered the leaf, offering a silent apology to the little plant. She hadn't realized how virulent the infection currently being drawn out of Chris was. She'd thought the plant would get a little sick, not start dying a mere four hours after she'd placed it there.

"You could have left."

She made a face at him. "I wouldn't leave a do...um, cat as

sick as you were, let alone a man."

He tried to laugh but it turned into a hacking cough.

Good. She handed him a paper towel. *Get it all out.* She held out a waste paper basket when he was done. She wasn't *that* altruistic. "Try and rest. Hopefully you'll feel better tonight." And if he didn't she'd have to find another plant.

He settled down with a sleepy sigh. "Thank you, Alannah."

She gave in to the urge to stroke his hair, feeling a stirring around her heart when he smiled sweetly. "You're welcome, Chris." She picked up the tray and left him to drift into a healing sleep.

She really hated invading his privacy, but she had to contact his family and let them know what was going on just in case he took a turn for the worse. She took his cell phone from his pants pocket and checked his voice mail. Luckily he had a model she was familiar with, and he hadn't put in a password.

The first message she heard had her sighing in relief. "Hey, Christopher, it's Gareth. Do me a favor and call me back once you get this. Bro, you're not going to believe what's been happening around here. Your mate called and told me you were kidnapping her. Wait until Mom hears about this."

Lana hoped she remembered correctly. She pressed speed dial three and waited for the connection.

"Hello?"

She'd gotten it right. The deep male voice on the other end of the line matched Gareth's. "This is Alannah Evans."

"The woman Christopher kidnapped? How's that going, by the way?"

"Long story. Look—"

"Have you accepted the mating?"

She growled. "What did Chris do, call you last night?"

"Uh..."

"Because I'm still not convinced of this whole perfect forever mate crap."

"Um..."

Lana began to pace. "He's a wizard!"

"Yeah, but—"

"I'm a witch." She shook her head. "It just can't work."

"It's going to have to."

She frowned. "What do you mean it's going to have to?"

"You answered the call, babe."

"Don't call me babe. And next time I'm letting my metaphysical answering machine get it."

He chuckled. "Too bad, so sad. You answered the call, making you a member of the Beckett pack, whether you like it or not."

"That's just it! I don't know if I like it or not."

"Does it bother you when he turns furry?" She made a rude noise, and he laughed. "Guess not. Have you two, um, 'done the deed' yet?"

"Ugh." She could practically hear the quotation marks.

"Seriously. Did he suck in bed? Is that why you're thinking of doing a flit?"

"First he drugged me, then he got sick off some spell we think someone named Cole used on him, and now I'm nursing him while he hacks up snot. Not exactly my idea of romance, let me tell you." There was no way in hell she was bringing up the workroom incident.

"Cole hexed him?"

Uh-oh. The teasing tone was completely gone from the other man's voice. "Let me guess. You're his *older* brother."

"Damn straight. Tell Christopher I'm on my way." Gareth hung up, leaving her holding a buzzing headset.

Lana hung up. "Lovely. Now I get to deal with two of them." At least Gareth had sounded like he knew who Cole was and how to deal with him. She stared at the phone before putting it where she'd originally found it, in Chris's pants. "And how does he know where we are, anyway?" She shook her head and decided to worry about it later. "Grammy!"

"Yes, dear?"

"Can I borrow the laptop?"

"Go right ahead. Pasta all right for dinner?"

"Does the Pope love Jesus?"

Grammy laughed and went back into the kitchen, shaking her head.

She headed into Grammy's bedroom and opened the laptop. *Big brother might know who Cole is, but I don't. And I'm the one he threatened to kill.* She booted up the computer, watching Windows come up. *The good Lord helps those who help themselves, and the Lady provides the means.* She settled down in the chair and began researching Christopher Beckett.

A half an hour later she had a better idea of who Christopher Beckett was, but was no closer to figuring out who Cole was. Chris was a graphic designer for Black Wolf Designs, a well-established firm in Pittsburgh. From his correspondence, they were responsible for the websites of some pretty major labels. The fact that his father was head of the firm explained the name of the company. She wondered why Chris had chosen to live so far outside his home city, but nothing in the Google search had answered her question.

Heading to the bookcase, she pulled down The Registry. Inside was listed the name of every wizard, witch and warlock around the world. Each copy was magically tied to a Master

Registry and updated when the Master updated.

How the Master updated was debatable. Some said one man was responsible, a scribe, priest or even a librarian who somehow magically knew when someone was born, died or had children, and added the information to The Registry. Others said it was secreted away in some far–off monastery, staffed by members of all three magical persuasions, all of them responsible for keeping the book updated. Still others believed the book updated when it needed to, with no interference from the mortals who referenced it or the person or persons who guarded it.

Lana believed the latter. To her it made perfect sense. Men could be bribed to alter registrations. Nothing could bribe the universe.

She opened the page to the Becketts, first checking out Christopher. She found his family listing easily. It seemed Chris had three brothers.

Gareth, the eldest by three years, and Daniel, two years younger than Chris, were both listed along with their prodigious bloodline. Both looked enough like Chris that they were unmistakably related.

But that wasn't the oddest part.

There was a short, not very informative entry for the youngest, Zachary Beckett. She wondered if he'd passed away, the entry was so brief. It was also rather strange, with a symbol on it she didn't see very often.

The wheel of Hecate.

She shivered. It was a symbol filled with both light and dark connotations, depending on how you interpreted it. On the one hand, the Goddess as Hecate was the Goddess of magic. Her chosen ones, called Hecate's Own, fought against the darkest of evils with powers other magic users could only dream of.

On the other, she was the Goddess of the Crossroads. The Goddess of death.

Simply seeing the wheel there could mean nothing more than Zach was deceased. But it could also mean so much more than that.

The Registry could be so vague at times.

She stretched, jumping at the sight of a strange man standing in the doorway of Grammy's bedroom. He had dark hair and golden eyes much like Chris did, but his features were harsher, less refined, and his hair was closer to dark brown than black. He looked a lot like the portrait of Gareth Beckett in The Registry.

"Lana? Your grandmother told me I could find you up here."

She grinned in relief at having her suspicions confirmed. "Gareth?"

He nodded and stepped forward to shake her hand. "Nice to meet you. Where's Christopher?"

"Bed, hopefully letting the remedies work."

His grin faded. "Remedies?"

She glared at him. The moment he started making fun of her witchy ways he was in for a world of hurt. "Don't start."

His lips twitched. "Yes, ma'am."

"We think this Cole person tied the sickness to some wolf hair Christopher somehow left behind last night."

"Tell me about it."

The command in his voice got her hackles up, but she could understand how he felt. It was his little brother in the other room sleeping off the effects of a nasty spell. "My car broke down last night."

"I got that, and I got you're Christopher's mate. How did Cole get a hold of some hair?"

"Cole was in the woods last night, and Chris tried to protect me."

"How did he protect you?"

She knew what he was *really* asking from the cautious way Gareth spoke. "His wolf jumped Cole."

"Which means the son of a bitch has hold of wolf fur. Fuck. Christopher can't shift or it'll get worse."

Lana smiled. "That's what I thought." Nice to have it confirmed.

"So you concocted something to help?"

"A plant in his room to draw the illness out and ground it into the earth, some ginger, anise and cinnamon tea, and chicken soup."

He blinked. "Chicken soup?"

She shrugged. Explaining the instinctive nature of a witch's magic to a wizard usually ended in frustration for both parties, and frankly she just wasn't up for explaining right now. "It's good for colds."

"Uh-huh." He shook his head. "I'm just going to go and check on Christopher." He nodded toward the computer. "Glad to see you're doing your homework."

She blushed at his knowing look but decided to brave it out. "Thanks."

Gareth Beckett strolled out of the room with the same grace his brother usually exhibited. Oddly the sight didn't move her the way it did when she watched Chris, but she still enjoyed the view. "How many of you are there, anyway?"

He was laughing. "Four."

"*Four* of you? Lord help the women of the world." She

frowned, glancing down at the open registry. *Wait. Four?* The Registry hinted that one of them had died.

Didn't it?

He ducked his head back in. "Only three of us are available now, babe."

"*Don't* call me babe." He made his way out of the office again, chuckling. "And who the hell *is* Cole, anyway?" She shouted after him.

"Ask Chris," he yelled in reply.

She rubbed her eyes with the heels of her hand, suddenly weary. "I'm so going to kill Kelly. Stupid boondock bachelorette party. It's not like there isn't a male strip club right here in Philly. We could have done pizza and Club Risqué, damn it." She turned to the computer and shot off a quick email to Kerry, telling her she'd get in touch as soon as she could, deleted the spam about a bigger penis for her pleasure, and shut the computer down before heading into the blue bedroom to face the Beckett brothers.

Time to throw myself to the wolves.

Chapter Eight

"Why are you here, Gareth?"

"Your mate didn't tell you I was on my way, did she?" Gareth was sprawled in the seat Lana had sat in, poking a curious finger at the mostly dead plant on the nightstand. Chris was vaguely reassured when he noticed there was still some green left on it. With Lana's help it might even survive.

"No, she didn't, probably because I was asleep up until ten minutes ago." Christopher got out of bed and reached for his shoes. He was feeling remarkably well considering he'd napped most of the day fully dressed. He usually felt rumpled and out of sorts on the rare occasions when that happened. Actually, he *did* still feel rumpled, but the knowledge his mate had chosen to stay by his side was a joyful hum inside him. He did, however, dislike feeling rumpled, so he decided to change into some fresh clothes.

"Hmm. Too busy on the computer, I guess."

Christopher stopped on the way to his suitcase. "She was probably just checking her email."

"And asking about Cole."

"Shit." Christopher ran his fingers through his hair. He'd been hoping she'd wait for him to deal with his old nemesis. He should have known better. "What did you tell her?" Because he already knew she'd take whatever little bone his brother had thrown her and build an entire skeleton out of it.

His brother shot him an annoyed look. "To ask you."

Christopher nodded, relieved. "Thanks."

"Don't mention it." Gareth grinned. "'Grats, by the way. Alannah's a cutie."

Christopher growled and grabbed his suitcase, heading into the bathroom in the hallway. He flipped open the suitcase and pulled out the nice dark-wash jeans. "Thank you. I think."

"Seriously. If you two weren't mated, I'd make a play for her. She's feisty."

Christopher pulled out the golden yellow microfiber shirt, wondering if Lana would like the soft feel of the fabric. He started to get undressed, tossing his dirty clothes into the suitcase. "Yes, she is. Almost too feisty."

"Hey, if she's too much for you to handle, bro, toss her my way. I could use a little cute and hot."

Christopher could feel his wolf protesting Gareth's laughing comment. "Drop it, Gareth." The rumbling quality of his voice startled him. The wolf was closer to the surface than he'd thought.

The silence on the other side of the door was deafening. Christopher got dressed and stepped back into the bedroom, ready to face his brother.

Instead he saw Lana sitting on the bed, Gareth staring out the window behind her. "Who's Cole?"

He finished buttoning his jeans, gratified at the way her gaze drifted to his hands. "Cole is a member of the Godwin family."

"The Godwins are rivals of the Becketts. They've hated us ever since great-great-great-great-granddad ate great-great-great-great-grandma." Gareth stretched and yawned. "Is anyone else hungry?"

Christopher just shook his head at Gareth. "It's a little more complicated."

Gareth shrugged. "Eh. Close enough."

Lana frowned. "The great-grandma who got eaten was a Godwin?"

"Yes, she was, and she was the reason our ancestor jilted the witch."

"And they *still* hold a grudge?"

Christopher shrugged. "Wizard memories are long."

"Do not meddle in the affairs of wizards, huh?"

"For you are crunchy and good with ketchup," Gareth snickered.

Christopher rolled his eyes. "That's dragons, nitwit."

Lana was looking at him with wide-eyed innocence. "Dragons are good with ketchup?"

He rolled his eyes. "Yes. Yes, they are. They are especially good on wheat buns."

"Sorry." But she didn't look repentant. He had the strongest urge to reach over and kiss the smile flirting at the edges of her mouth.

"Cole, for some bizarre reason, felt the need to poke at Christopher all through school." Gareth moved away from the window and sprawled in the chair next to the bed.

Christopher almost growled. Gareth's knee was touching Lana's. He reached out and moved her leg. "And I, for one, didn't really see why I shouldn't poke back."

"This great rivalry sprung up between them."

He sat next to Lana, placing one hand on her knee, knowing how possessive the move looked and not really caring.

He *was* possessive where she was concerned, so everyone would just have to get used to it. "Things got more and more heated. Competing for the same grades, the same classes—"

"The same girls." Christopher snarled at Gareth, who just grinned. "Seriously, bro, my favorite was when you marked Cole's backpack in college."

"Marked? You mean...?"

Gareth nodded. "Yup. And it was open at the time."

Christopher flushed. Gareth still, after all these years, found it hilariously funny, and brought it up every chance he got.

"Ugh." Lana shuddered, looking disgusted. He'd have to explain to her later exactly how drunk he'd been when he'd done it. "But why did Cole threaten to kill me? So far it sounds more like jealousy than anything else. What drove it over the edge of pissy testosterone games into death threats?"

"He threatened to *kill you?*" Gareth stood, his hair practically standing on end, and glared at Chris. "When were you going to tell me Cole threatened your mate?"

"I would have last night, but you were too busy laughing your ass off over the fact I'd mated a witch."

Gareth zipped his lips. "Ixnay on the aughinglay."

"Oronmay."

Lana's comeback startled a laugh out of Gareth. "I *like* her."

The hand on Lana's knee tightened. "Just don't like her too much."

Gareth waved his hand. "Maybe I'll mate a witch. They're a lot more fun than some of those prissy wizard women."

"Uh-huh." Lana stood and brushed by Gareth. "Okay, so Cole wants to get even with Christopher for peeing on his life, right?"

"Something like that." Christopher found himself not surprised at all when she started pacing. It looked to be a habit of hers when she was thinking or upset.

"It was something more, actually." Christopher glared at Gareth, but Gareth kept going. "Christopher stole Cole's fiancée."

"Oh." Lana was glaring at him. "How could you steal another man's fiancée?"

"First, she didn't tell me she was engaged."

"People say you could hear the sounds of her having a *really* good time on the entire dorm floor." Gareth sighed.

Christopher tried to ignore his brother, focusing instead on Lana. "Second, you can't *steal* another human being."

Gareth grinned wickedly. "I understand she was a screamer."

Christopher gritted his teeth against the urge to strangle his brother. "Third, when I found out she was engaged to Cole I went to him and apologized."

"I heard one guy actually came out of his room and started waving a ruler like he was conducting a symphony." Gareth, glancing sideways at Christopher, waved his hands to an imaginary beat.

Too much more and Gareth would find himself flung out the window headfirst. "Cole decided to fight me. He was humiliated when I won."

"Then there was this other girl who—"

"Gareth. Don't make me kill you. Mom would get pissed."

Lana was wiping at her mouth, but she couldn't hide her grin. "Okay. So Cole wants to hurt me in order to hurt you. I get it. He must not have thought I could take him."

"You can't." Gareth's face paled, the humor replaced by

93

horror.

Hell, so did Christopher's. The speculation in her eyes scared the crap out of him. "He's a wizard, sweetheart. He'll be prepared to face another wizard."

She cocked her hip and frowned. "So?"

"Mom taught us that witches were very powerful, but only if strong emotion was behind what they did."

She nodded. "Like the witch who cursed your family."

"Yes. And wizards are more like chess players, planning every move way in advance, prepared for every eventuality."

She smirked. "Other than being cursed into werewolves."

Chris blinked. "Well, yes. Although I understand it's become standard practice to guard against similar curses."

She rolled her eyes. "Can't imagine why."

Christopher cleared his throat. "A wizard's strength is less fluid, but requires less power at the end since we've already got the spells in place. They just require a trigger. A witch might hold a wizard off for a little while, but I believe the wizard would ultimately win because he'd have more power at his disposal."

"I think you believe it because you've never faced a pissed-off witch before."

He took her hands in his. "You don't understand."

"Then show me. I mean, didn't I break the sickness spell? I think I can take a wizard."

He blinked. She couldn't seriously be asking... "No."

"Why not?"

He squeezed her hands, horrified at the very idea. "No way in hell will I duel you."

She sniffed. "You're just afraid I'll win."

"Uh, guys?"

Christopher was outraged. "I do not think you'll win! I would kick your ass."

"You *so* would not, Scooby."

"Guys?"

"Oh, I think I would!" He huffed. *Scooby?* He owed her for that one.

"Please. All I'd have to do is wave a Milk Bone around and you'd be toast."

Gareth got between them, holding up both hands. "Don't you two think it's a bit more important to figure out why Cole wants you dead?"

"Good question." Christopher still wasn't certain what had pushed Cole over the edge. He hadn't been near the man in two years, and last time had been cold, but civil.

Lana rolled her eyes. "Like I haven't been asking the same thing."

"Yesterday he threatened Lana. Unless I miss my guess the little head cold he gave Christopher was meant to be a great deal more uncomfortable than it turned out to be."

Christopher lifted Lana's hand to his lips. "Thanks to you." He kissed her fingers, loving the soft blush on her cheeks.

"You're welcome." She took her hand out of his and resumed her pacing. "But we still don't know what's going on. I could see him trying to seduce me, or take me away for revenge, but murder?"

Christopher studied Lana. His little witch had hit on what had been bothering him since yesterday. "She's right. Something much bigger is going on here." Christopher reached out and stroked one of the few green leaves left on the plant. "Something Cole is willing to kill for."

"I got nothing." Lana rubbed wearily at her eyes. Across the kitchen Gareth was talking to someone on the phone, his voice low and urgent. In front of her, the laptop's screen remained depressingly empty of answers.

Christopher handed her a can of soda with a weary sigh. "I've tried scrying, but Cole is blocked. And divining doesn't seem to be getting me anywhere either." He scrubbed at his face with his free hand. "It doesn't help that most of my equipment is back at my house."

She smiled, opening the can of soda. "Maybe your tarot cards are broke. Want to borrow mine?"

"No, thanks." He sat down next to her, casually draping an arm around her shoulders. He gently stroked her hair. "Head hurt?"

Without even thinking about it she leaned into his touch. She'd always loved having her hair played with. "A little."

Grammy came into the kitchen, her phone in her hand. "I've put out feelers among the witches. It's a long shot, but maybe someone in our community has heard of or had dealings with Cole and can give us a clue what he's up to." She joined Lana and Chris at the kitchen table and put the phone down with a sigh. "Any luck?"

Lana shook her head. "Nope."

"Darn."

"I think I might know." Gareth joined them at the table, looking a little wild-eyed. "It seems the king is considering naming his successor."

"And?" Lana took a sip of her coke.

"Rumor has it one of the people he's considering is a Beckett."

Lana choked. Christopher pounded her gently on the back. "And let me guess who the other person he's considering is."

"A Godwin." Lana groaned. "Crap. Why focus on Chris, though?"

"Cole has always seen Chris as his greatest competition, but there's no saying Chris is the Beckett being considered, or that Cole is the Godwin."

"Then we need to confirm it one way or the other." Chris continued stroking her hair, soothing her despite the topic.

"So why go after me? Was it to lure Chris out?" The two men exchanged looks that had every hair on the back of her neck standing on end. "What are you two not telling me?"

"Whoa, look at the time!" Gareth stood and drained his iced tea. "Gotta run! Is there a hotel nearby I can stay at?"

Grammy glared at him and pointed. "Sit." The power in her voice was unmistakable.

Gareth, looking startled, sat abruptly.

"*Speak.*"

"Gareth—" The warning in Chris's voice startled her.

The karmic backlash from forcing Gareth to speak could be bad, but it was too late. Grammy had spoken, therefore Gareth would speak. "Now that Lana has answered the call, Chris's life force is tied to hers. If she dies or ultimately rejects him, Chris will slowly fade away."

Lana's jaw dropped. "Are you telling me if I don't *mate* with him he'll *die*?"

Chris winced. "Alannah..."

"It's literally a life-and-death fuck?"

"*Alannah!*"

It was Lana's turn to wince. "Sorry, Grammy." She turned

to Chris and smacked him on the arm. "When were you going to tell me this?"

He was glaring at Gareth, who looked horrified. "I wasn't."

"Why not?"

He turned his attention back to her, his expression softening. "Because I wanted you to choose *me*, not my life."

"What if I had said no?"

"You could still say no." His finger brushed over her cheek.

He had *to be kidding, right?* "God, now my head *really* hurts." There was no way she could live with herself if Chris died simply because she said no, but she wasn't ready to say yes yet no matter how much his touch made her cream her panties or how good the sex was. They were living in a bubble, but when the real world inserted itself into their lives he'd see he *must* have made a mistake. No wizard family would tolerate having a witch in it!

He frowned immediately, getting up from the table to find the Tylenol. "Here, take this. You want something to eat?"

The milk, four glasses and a plate of Oreos floated onto the table. "Dig in." Grammy grabbed and cookie and twisted it apart, licking the cream inside. "What?"

It was no use berating her grandmother for using her powers the way she had. Grammy knew the consequences probably better than Lana did. Lana picked up a cookie and bit into it.

Gareth shook his head. "Here, let me." He poured them each a glass of milk, handing them around. "We have to decide what to do about this before Cole tries again."

"We've neutralized the sickness spell. I doubt he has enough fur to try anything more." Chris dunked his cookie twice before shoving half of it into his mouth.

"And even if he did, Grammy and I spelled the soup to make sure it wouldn't take." The brothers stared at her. "What, you've never heard of preventative medicine?" She swallowed the Tylenol, chasing it with another bite of Oreo. *Yum. My kind of medicine.*

"I didn't hear you spellcasting."

"You wouldn't have." Grammy took another Oreo. "I don't know exactly how a wizard's magic works, but words aren't always necessary for a witch to cast a spell. It's the symbol they represent, the stated intent behind the spell that's important. Visualization can work wonders, especially when a sick person is involved."

Gareth pointed at Lana, a slow grin crossing his face. "That's why you gave him chicken soup!"

She shrugged and dunked her next cookie. "I told you, it's good for colds."

Chapter Nine

Lana woke up the next morning to a feeling of warmth. A heavy arm lay across her stomach, another under her head. She could feel Chris curled up behind her, spooning her, his breath gently stirring her hair.

"Chris?"

A snore was her answer.

"Chris?"

A deep breath huffed out, blowing her bangs into her eyes. She would have reached up and brushed them away but her arm was trapped under his.

"Chris!"

"Huh?" She turned her head to find sleepy gold eyes staring down at her. "Mornin'."

"Why are you in my bed?"

He reached up and brushed her hair away from her eyes. "Because Gareth's sleeping in *my* bed."

She glared at him. "This isn't Goldilocks."

"Guess I can't call you Teddy then." He snuggled into the blanket, tugging her closer. "Go back to sleep."

"I said separate bedrooms, Chris."

"Yup. I have a bedroom."

She nudged him with her elbow. "Go sleep in it."

"But someone else is sleeping in my bed." He pouted down at her, all sleep rumpled. His voice was a sleepy rumble, melting her insides into aroused goo. It took all of her willpower to keep from pressing her rear end against his hot erection, but after sampling him the other day, it was much harder than she thought.

Mm, much, much *harder.* She shook her head, trying to get visions of riding him in reverse cowgirl out of her head. "You've never shared a bedroom with your brother before?"

"Bedroom, yes. Bed, no. He hogs the covers and he snores, but the worst part? He tried to snuggle and called me Tammy."

Lana choked. "No way."

Chris shuddered. "Trust me. It was leave or face deflowering."

"Look on the bright side. He didn't call you *Tommy* while being all cuddly."

Chris whimpered. "Are you *trying* to break my brain?"

She giggled.

"What time is it?" He rolled over slightly, checking the glowing numbers on the clock. "Six thirty? You're a *morning person?*"

She giggled again.

"You can't be a morning person. No way would fate be that cruel."

"Unlike you, I have a boss who expects me at work in the mornings."

He buried his face in her hair. "Please tell me you at least make coffee."

"Is there anything else people drink in the morning?"

He sighed happily. "Okay, I forgive you." He placed a kiss on the top of her head. "Hey, Nurse Evans? I have this pain."

She smacked his hip. "Go back to sleep, perv."

"Don't you want to take my temperature?" He gave her puppy-dog eyes, but his wandering hands were anything but puppy-like. His fingers were between her legs, stroking in slow, seductive circles.

"Chris?"

"Hmm?"

"You have to let go so I can get up."

"One of us is up already."

"Chris!"

He rolled on top of her, his cock resting against her opening. "You're a morning person, remember?"

She licked her lips, the feel of his warm body drugging her. "I told myself no more surprise sex."

One brow rising, he slowly thrust against her, nudging her entrance. "There's no surprise here, Lana. We already know how good it can be." He bent over her with a warm smile. "I promise you." He licked her chin, the move surprisingly erotic. "This time?" He nipped her earlobe, pulling a shudder from her. "It will be better."

She gulped. Her resistance was melting like butter in the sun. "Better?"

"Mmm." The purring growl sent a shiver through her. "I plan on taking my time." He kissed the hollow of her throat. "I want to savor every inch of you." He tasted the top of her left breast. "Find out what makes you shiver." He sucked her nipple into aching hardness. One finger thrust into her pussy, stroking her in time with the suction of his mouth. She gasped, arching

102

up into his hand and mouth. His thumb stroked over her clit with every thrust, bringing it to painful life. "I want to know what makes you scream, and how to get you to whimper."

"I shouldn't." She fucked herself on his finger, fighting her body's desires. Her body was winning, clubbing her fears to death with strong, steady strokes of one male finger. And who the hell was she kidding? She shouldn't, but she was going to!

He chuckled. "You should. You definitely should." He slipped under the comforter. Before she could even squeak, his warm tongue was lapping at her pussy. Over and over, gentle then hard, from her hole to her clit.

That was the last straw. Her brain threw its hands up in disgust and took a back seat to her libido. "Lick me. God, lick me." She threaded her fingers through his hair, her fingers stroking, encouraging him. She'd given up her half-hearted protest in favor of the incredible sensations he was pulling from her body. He methodically stroked her with his tongue, his sighs and moans showing exactly how much he was enjoying his task. When her hips began moving, he encouraged her, his lapping tongue moving faster and faster until she was fucking his face, eager for the orgasm just on the edge of her senses. When it hit, she bucked up against him with a groan.

But he didn't stop. He kept licking, kept sucking until her hips were moving again, her fingers clutching in his hair. Another, stronger orgasm started to build, frightening her with how badly she wanted it. She felt something enter her and knew from the stretch he'd added some fingers, fucking in and out of her, driving the sensations even higher.

"Fuck me, fuck me, fuck me." She could hear herself chanting softly, barely aware of what she was saying.

In answer he pulled her clit into his mouth, strumming it lightly until she was gasping her pleasure, the orgasm so strong her entire body bowed around his head, her fingers tightening in his hair until it had to hurt.

He waited until she sank down onto the mattress before prowling up her body. Once again the irises of his eyes were swallowed by the pupils, making his eyes appear black rimmed in gold. It was the sexiest fucking thing she'd ever seen.

He thrust hard, powering into her. This time it was his hands clenching in her hair. He pulled her head back, using her body with each and every powerful thrust of his cock. He growled softly and buried his face in her neck, biting hard enough to suck up a mark, his hips snapping faster and faster against her.

Once again she was going to come. It was building, higher and higher, his cock brushing the incredible spot inside her with each pounding drive into her body. She wrapped her legs around him, pulling him into her, grimacing when his hands tightened and pulled her head even farther to the side, exposing her vulnerable neck.

He picked another spot, biting and sucking, growling long and low against her, his cock moving so fast she knew he was about to come. She wasn't far behind him, but this time she was determined he would go first. His panting breaths fanned her neck. "God. Love. Coming. Come. My witch. *Mine.*"

Without thought she reached down and stroked her clit, her fingers brushing against the base of his wet cock. With a strangled moan he came, jerking against her in short, stabbing strokes.

She let go, her own orgasm washing over her in blinding waves, her body clutching his like it never wanted to let him go.

Chris slowly lowered himself beside her, his cock slipping out of her with a wet sound. "I think I could get used to a morning person." He grinned at her, his chest heaving, his arm draping around her waist.

She shook her head at him, feeling too good to take issue with the male satisfaction on his face. Besides, making her come three times? She figured he deserved a little smugness. She glanced at the clock and winced. "I hate to tell you this but I have to get up."

He snuggled into her, his knee between her thighs, his head on her chest. "No, you don't."

"Yes, I do, you big baby. I have to go to work."

"Call out sick."

"Can't. I have a big project due today."

"But you're so warm," he grumbled.

"Chris!"

"Fine." He huffed, but he let her go, rolling onto his back with a pout.

"I'll see you after work, you big baby."

"Mm-hmm." He was already curling up around her pillow. "Smells good."

With a sigh, he slid back into sleep. She couldn't help the smile crossing her face. "Sleep tight, wolfman." She leaned over and kissed his forehead. "I like you too."

Christopher woke to the sound of a loud thud. He stretched, grateful for the extra sleep Lana had—

"Get *off* me, you big ape!"

Christopher lurched out of bed, grabbed his jeans, and began shoving his legs into them. Lana sounded pissed, but worse, she sounded scared.

"What in hell is wrong with you?" Gareth was bellowing like

a wounded bull. "You want to wind up a smear on the landscape?"

Gareth? What the fuck was he doing to scare Lana? Christopher was at the bedroom door pulling it open when Lana screeched. "Let *go* of me!"

He thundered barefoot down the stairs just in time to see Gareth land on the floor, hands cradling his balls. "What the fuck is going on?"

Gareth was rolling around on the floor, his face a rictus of agony. "Owww."

Lana flipped her hair over her shoulders, glaring at Gareth. "He grabbed hold of me and threatened to tie me up!"

"She was going to go to work!"

Christopher crossed his arms over his chest and glared at them both. "Work?"

"I wasn't leaving the house!" Lana threw her hands up in the air and flounced onto the living room sofa. "I realized over breakfast it would be too dangerous to go into the office, so I called work and told them I needed to telecommute for the next couple of days." She waved her hand toward Gareth, who was just picking himself gingerly up off the floor. "Doofus over there saw me heading for the staircase to tell you what was going on, thought I was leaving the house and assaulted me."

"I did not attack you!"

"You picked me up off the floor and threatened to tie me up!"

Christopher shook his head and headed past Gareth into the kitchen. It was too damn early in the morning to listen to his mate and his brother bickering without the fortification of caffeine. Besides, he bet Gareth had done exactly what Lana said he'd done. Big brother could be more than overprotective at times. He could be a real pain in the ass.

Christopher tried to look on the bright side. At least he knew if anything happened to him, Lana would be well guarded. The volume of the fight increased. He could hear Gareth threatening to stuff Lana in a closet for her own safety.

He winced. *Very well guarded.*

"Good morning, Chris. Need a mug?"

"Good morning, Annabelle. I would love a mug, thank you."

She smiled serenely, ignoring Lana's voice threatening to do more than just kick Gareth's prized jewels if he ever laid a hand on her again. "Sugar? Cream?"

Christopher took a seat at the banquette and absently scratched his chest, stifling a yawn. "Yes, please. Do I smell Danishes?"

She put the mug in front of him, her expression merry. "Yes, in fact you do. Lemon, cherry or cheese?"

He picked up his mug and took a sip. "God, that's good. Cheese, please, and thank you."

"You're a polite one. I like it." She brought him a Danish and joined him at the table. They ate peacefully despite the battle raging on in the front of the house. He picked up the newspaper lying on the table, opening it to the sports section, settling in for a nice breakfast.

"Ugh! Your brother is impossible." Lana stomped in and poured herself a cup of coffee.

"Yes, dear." Christopher turned to the financial pages, handing Gareth the sports section.

"I am not impossible, you're impossible." Gareth stole Christopher's mug, frowning when he saw it was empty.

"I didn't play grabby with anyone." She bit savagely into a Danish, glaring at Gareth.

107

"No, you just kicked me in my—" he darted a quick look at Annabelle, "—man parts."

"You were holding me up in the air and refusing to let go. What was I supposed to do?"

"*Not* kick me in my man parts? That would have been a good start."

"How about next time you not assume you know what I'm up to?" Lana crossed her arms over her chest and glared at Gareth.

The mug got slammed down on the table. "You die, my brother dies. What part of this do you not get?" Gareth stood. "I'm going for a walk." He stomped out of the room. Seconds later they heard the front door slam.

Lana collapsed against the countertop. "He needs to switch to decaf." She settled onto the bench next to Christopher. "Good morning." She kissed him on the cheek, her lips sticky from the Danish.

Christopher held still for a moment, shocked. It was the first affectionate gesture she'd shown toward him on her own, and he was stunned by it. "Good morning."

"You want more coffee?" She took his mug and stood, pouring him a cup, refreshing her own. "Another Danish?"

He looked over at Annabelle. "When did we replace my mate with a Stepford wife?"

"Ha ha." She sat next to him. "I have to log in about thirty...no, twenty minutes now. Anything interesting in the paper?"

"Other than the Flyers winning last night, not really." He smiled to himself when Annabelle winked and left the kitchen. "Now, how about a proper good morning?" He slid his hand around her waist and pulled her in closer to him. Her pleased look was distinctly feminine, full of secrets he was dying to uncover. He gave her a sweet, slow kiss, exploring her mouth, tasting the flavor of cherry and woman. "Mmm. Good morning."

"Good morning."

"I really need to ask this for obvious reasons. Does kicking a man in the balls always put you in this good a mood?"

She laughed. "No. I just...started thinking about what you and Gareth both said last night." She put her arms around his neck and sighed. "I need to figure out how to accept this whole mate call thingy you Becketts do. When my car broke down during the storm? I had the feeling it was the Lady trying to tell me something. When Cole was in those woods chasing me, I knew safety was in front of me, and when I saw the wolf I knew I'd found it. Add in everyone telling me I was the answer to your prayers and I know I need to try and work through this."

He couldn't help it. He stole another kiss, grateful beyond belief she was willing to give them a chance. "Thank you."

"Once this whole Cole thing is over we're going on a *real* date. Understood? Just because you didn't pay your dollar for the marriage lottery like everyone else doesn't mean you get out of wining and dining me, got it?"

"Do I get to seduce you too?"

She bit her lip, a slight flush to her cheeks, her eyes full of promise. "Maybe. If you play your cards right."

He leaned in and took one more kiss. He could easily get addicted to the taste of her mouth. "At least I won't be playing solitaire anymore."

She wrinkled her nose at him. "That was bad, wolfman."

He shrugged. "The caffeine hasn't kicked in yet."

She shook her head and pulled away from him with flattering reluctance. "Time to go to work."

"Bring the laptop into the living room. I'll set mine up there too and we can work together." He followed her out of the kitchen, enjoying the sight of her ass swaying lazily in front of him.

"How do you know I'm not on the phone all day long?"

Huh. What does *she do for a living?* With how quickly everything had happened in the last two days he'd forgotten to ask. "I don't?"

She snorted, heading up the stairs. He followed after pausing for a moment to enjoy the view. "You're lucky, because I'm not."

"What *do* you do?"

She looked up at him with a smirk. "I'm an accountant."

He stumbled. Somehow regimented numbers and tax laws didn't really fit in with his vision of her. "Really?"

She wiggled her fingers at him from the bedroom door. "They say I'm magic with numbers."

"Ouch." He headed for his bedroom and grabbed his laptop case. Gareth might have stolen his bed but at least he knew better than to touch Chris's laptop.

"Who do you need to get in touch with over the whole king business?"

"Not sure. I'll fire off an email to my father, have him look into what's going on. Meanwhile I need to get some work done too. Do you mind music?"

She paused, putting the laptop down on the coffee table. "In general, no. Why?"

"I like to work with some playing in the background." It helped set the mood for the work he was doing.

"You have headphones?" She sank gracefully to the floor, getting to hands and knees to plug the laptop in.

That luscious ass of hers was up in the air and she expected him to speak human? The memory of the incredible sex they'd shared had him so hard he was surprised there was any blood left in his head. He figured there must be *some* left there though. He was still breathing.

She rolled her eyes when she saw where his gaze had landed. "Head. Phones." Each word was accompanied by a wiggle of her ass.

He gulped. He hadn't thrown his underwear on under his jeans, and now he was going to have a permanent zipper mark up his cock. "Uh." He was *definitely* going to have to fuck her in that position. *Note to self: Pick up lube.* He wondered if she'd let him talk her into taking her there.

He bet he could. After all, he'd already had her twice when she'd been unsure. If she'd given him a firm no either time, he'd have backed off, threat of blue balls or not. But she hadn't. She'd given so sweetly, come so beautifully for him, he was permanently addicted.

"I'll take that as a yes." She sat up, sitting on her heels and holding out her hand. "There. Hand me your plug."

He blinked. It took him a second to realize she meant the *electrical* plug. *She'd look so incredible with her ass plugged.* "Here."

She plugged in his laptop, giving him another show. "All done. The travel surge protector I had should work for now." She squirmed around, sitting cross-legged in front of the laptop. She looked up at him with a grin, her eyes drifting lazily over his erection. "Work now, play later."

He sat down so hard he nearly bounced. "Work. Then play. Got it." He stared at the blank screen. "What was I working on?"

She leaned over and whispered in his ear, "Turning on the laptop."

He stared down at the top of her head, trying to ignore the way her shoulders shook with her laughter. *It's going to be a long day.*

Chapter Ten

Lana reached up with her arms and stretched, her back feeling stiff from sitting on the floor. She leaned against the sofa, pushing her legs under the coffee table. Chris's music track had gone from Joe Satriani to Enya, the soft strains filling the room, his mouse moving in sweeping arcs across the mouse pad. "Wouldn't it be easier with one of those drawing pads I've heard about?"

"Considerably, but I forgot to pack it."

"Oh." She stood up, more than ready for a bio break. "Want anything to drink?"

"Coke?"

"I can do that." She headed for the tiny powder room, relieving herself before heading to the kitchen. She grabbed two cans out of the fridge and slammed the door shut. She then promptly screeched.

Gareth winced. "Sorry."

Lana put her hand to her chest. "Fuck, Gareth, you trying to kill me?"

He had his hands shoved in his pockets and a sheepish expression on his face. "I'm sorry if I overreacted this morning."

She handed him one of the Cokes and opened the fridge door, grabbing another one. "In that case I'm sorry I racked you."

He winced and followed her out of the kitchen. "I can tell my future mate our children are little mutants because of you."

"No blaming me for your wizardlings, dude." She sat down on the floor, handing Chris his soda.

Gareth snorted and stepped over her, plopping himself on the sofa. "Hey, bro."

Chris grunted, sweeping some magenta onto his design.

"Isn't he just a little ray of sunshine when he's working?"

Chris lifted his hand from the mouse long enough to give Gareth the bird.

"Ah, sibling love. Makes me glad I'm an only child." She toasted them with her can before popping the top.

"Wait until you meet the rest of the family."

Chris looked up, a frown on his face. "Do you two mind? I'm trying to work."

"Sorry. So sorry." Lana stood and tiptoed out of the room, making shushing noises at Gareth and bowing to Chris whenever he looked up. The reluctant amusement on his face made her overly dramatic posturing worthwhile.

She headed into the kitchen again, intent on making sandwiches. Maybe feeding some meat to her grumpy wolf would tame him a bit.

Grammy came up from the basement, a look of concern on her face.

"What is it?" Lana asked.

"I heard from someone high up in the witches' council."

Uh-oh. "And?"

"It's confirmed. The wizard king is gravely ill. None of their healing spells are working. He wants to name his successor before he passes on, and he's definitely considering someone from either the Becketts or the Godwins." She shook her head sadly. "He even went so far to ask one of our specialists to look at him, but there was nothing we could do for him. Poor man."

"Do they know who he's thinking of naming?"

"We're been scrying all day, but so far none of us has been able to come up with anything."

"Which means either he hasn't decided himself or he's blocking any magical attempts to find out."

Grammy nodded, grabbing the bread. "It makes sense. You can't mess with the game if you don't know all the players. I'm certain the other rulers would do the same." She sighed, the bread dropping onto the plate. Lana took a good look at her, just noticing the dark circles under Grammy's eyes. "I'm too tired to cook tonight, sweetheart. Do you mind sandwiches?"

Lana thought about ordering in pizza but reluctantly decided against it. She had no idea if Cole knew where they were yet and she wasn't willing to take chances. There were so many things he could do to the pizza, or the delivery man, that fell into the not good category. "I've already started making them. Why don't you let me finish? Have a seat."

"Thank you, dear. I will." Grammy settled wearily onto the bench.

Lana called the men in to grab the sandwiches once they were done. Chris entered first, the frown of concentration gone from his face. He was even smiling. Lana saw Gareth wink at her before Chris swooped down, planting a hearty kiss on her cheek. "Did you have a good day at work, dear?"

She snorted. "Not too bad. You?"

"I had a very good day. There was this cute new girl in the office. I swear, I think she flirted with me a few times." He was grinning down at her, cradling her body in his arms, swaying gently against her. But something manic was in his eyes, something wild and untamed.

"Really? Do I need to be worried about her?" She studied him closely, worried by what she saw.

He shrugged. "Nah. You're much cuter, and you smell better." He sniffed her neck, laughing when she playfully slapped his chest. He turned his head, his grin turning savage when he saw the sandwiches. "Roast beef." He reached over and grabbed one, shoving half into his mouth in one go.

"Ew." Lana stepped back. "Slow down, Captain Carnivore. You might choke on the gristle."

Chris looked shocked for a moment before swallowing hard, making a weird face. She thought maybe the beef got briefly stuck halfway down. Not surprising since she usually packed half a cow on her sandwiches. "Sorry."

Gareth sighed. "I need a run too."

The brothers exchanged glances. "Where?" Chris sat, pulling Lana into his lap and handing her a sandwich. "Eat." When she squirmed to get more comfortable, he growled, tightening his arms around her waist. It was like he thought she was trying to get away. She settled down, hoping it would calm her wolfman down.

"No place around here is safe. We'd have to head out of the city a ways. Thanks." Gareth smiled sweetly at Grammy when she passed him the lemonade, but his expression remained troubled.

"Do you two need to change every day?" Lana bit delicately into her sandwich. Rich tomato and tangy mustard burst over her tongue. *Yummy.* She hadn't realized how hungry she'd been until she'd taken a bite. The moment she did the low-level grumble rattling Chris's chest ceased, and his big body eased.

What the hell?

"I wouldn't go more than three days without changing. Things can get, pardon the pun, hairy if we don't." Chris dropped a kiss on her shoulder. "It's been a while since I've had to deal with it. We might not be able to stay here too much longer."

He sounded genuinely regretful. Considering the circumstances she couldn't find it in her to call him on it. He was looking really uncomfortable. She decided to put him out of his misery. "To your place then?"

"I think so." He rubbed his hand up and down her back. "I'm sorry, Lana. I should have thought of this. I wish I didn't have to break my promise to you."

She kissed his cheek, hoping to ease some more of the tension in him. "Don't worry about it. I'm sure there are some perks to dating a werewolf."

"Like?" He settled her more securely on his lap. She could feel his erection growing under her bottom, a different hunger lighting his eyes.

"Hmm. Never having cold feet in bed again?"

Gareth laughed. "Yup, that's the biggest perk all right."

She put the sandwich down on the plate and wrapped her arms around Chris's neck, focusing on him. "And you already come housetrained."

His lips twitched. "True."

"And if you chew my shoes you can afford to replace them."

He looked ready to burst, either in laughter or indignation, she couldn't tell which. "I am *not* a poodle."

"Well, that's good. I'm not really into yappy dogs." She ran her hand teasingly down his chest and used her best seductive voice. "I like *real* dogs."

Gareth's head was on the table, his shoulders shaking.

Chris was still fighting a laugh when his cell phone rang. "Hello?" The tension she'd managed to almost eradicate once more tightened his shoulders, the laughter fleeing from his face. "What do you want, Cole?" She tried to hear what was being said but couldn't. All she could hear was a soft murmuring voice, but the tone came through loud and clear, the menace in the sounds dripping from the speaker. Chris's eyes narrowed, his mouth tightening at whatever Cole was saying. "You *really* don't want to do that, Cole. Trust me." The last words were said in a low growl shivers sped down her spine. Her wolfman was getting seriously pissed off.

When his eyes darted to Grammy, it was Lana's turn to stiffen. *"What?"* She mouthed, hoping he'd be able to give her an answer.

"The Evans family is off limits. Don't threaten them again. Do you understand me?" He listened for a moment, his hand tightening painfully on her hip, his gaze boring into hers. "What makes you think he'll pick you once he finds out you've been threatening innocent bystanders? Cole? *Cole!* Damn it!" He closed the phone and tossed it onto the table. "We have to leave tonight. He's not only found out who you are but where we are." The look he exchanged with Gareth worried her. "He said to tell you hi."

"Damn. He's stronger than I thought." Lana shivered, grateful when Chris pulled her close, burying her face in his neck. "Can he hurt Grammy?"

His arms tightened around her. "I'll protect you both. You have my word on it."

She didn't even have to think over everything he'd already done to protect her. "I know." The soft wonder in his face was worth her show of trust. She smiled and fed him a bit of sandwich. *Hmm. Maybe we can work this out after all.*

It didn't take long to get everything packed into the car. Gareth volunteered to drive Annabelle, leaving Christopher alone with his mate and a burning need to let the wolf free. The two women exchanged quick hugs, and they were off, heading back to Christopher's house and the problems that hadn't gone away. If anything, the new threat Cole had obliquely uttered had upped the stakes considerably. Lana would never forgive herself, or him, if anything happened to Annabelle.

And still, the only thing he could think about was his need to rip his clothing off his body and run until he collapsed.

Damn it, how could he have forgotten? Most days it wasn't a problem, because he'd made sure it wasn't one. He'd even gone to a college in the suburbs, living in a place with a good wooded area behind it for short runs. It was a lesson he'd learned from his parents. His relatives might work in the city but they *lived* outside it.

Now, thanks to his illness, he hadn't run in two days, and the wolf was anxious to get out of its cage. The only reason he could think of for the wolf to be so itchy to get out was the fact they had yet to fully claim their mate. "Once we're back at the house, Gareth and I will be going for a run."

"All right." She put her hand on his thigh, the warmth of her seeping through the rough denim. Suddenly his wolf's urges were heading in a completely different direction, one that had his cock rock hard enough to drill holes in steel. "Is there anything I can do to help?"

He could think of a few things she could do. Unzipping his fly, lowering her head, taking his prick out of his pants, sucking it into the warm cavern of her mouth...

"Chris? You might want to pull over."

He looked at her. "Why?"

She gestured with her chin toward the steering wheel.

119

"Your hands are sprouting fur."

"Fuck." He pulled over. Luckily they'd already left the city, but they were still on a major highway. He leaned his head against the seat, closing his eyes and taking deep breaths.

He couldn't understand it. He should have more control than this.

Her hand tried to leave his thigh. His growling response startled even him. "Chris?"

The fear in her voice nearly killed him. He reached for the door handle, ignoring her when she reached into her purse, determined to get away from her before his wolf got the better of him. He was terrified of what he would do to her if it should happen.

She reached out and began to stroke his hair, freezing him in his tracks.

"Artemis who guards the night

Aid us now in our plight.

Man and beast within collide;

Bring forth the man to guide.

By your hand, by my decree.

As I will so mote it be."

She pressed something into the palm of his hand, stroking his fingers over it, using her own to guide him, her other still tangled in his hair. Her quiet chant continued, her soft voice something both he and the wolf could focus on. The feel of the cool stone helped center him, guided the man once more to the surface and dominance.

"Lana?"

"Shh. It's okay, Chris. I've got you." Sweat beaded her brow, her voice tired. "This wasn't natural, Chris."

He ground his teeth. *Fucking Cole again. There must have been more of the wolf hair than I thought.*

"He must have held back some of the wolf hairs from the earlier spell."

"He was trying to force the wolf out, tried to nullify the contract we have with it."

She shook her head. "I don't think he can. I think he did try to bring out your wolf, but it wouldn't have hurt me. I'm sure of it."

He wasn't. She hadn't felt the raw hunger his wolf had blasted him with. But the wolf lay docile now under her palm, ready to beg for more caresses from his mate.

He opened his fingers and stared down at the milky white gem in his hand. "Moonstone?"

"I invoked Artemis." She grinned wearily. "And you *are* a werewolf."

He snorted, too tired to argue with her. "I'm sorry if I scared you."

Her fingers shifted, closing his around the moonstone again. "I think you scared yourself more than you scared me." She shifted in her seat. "Are you all right to drive?"

He nodded. Already he could feel his strength returning. "Yeah, I think so."

"Good." She yawned. "Wake me when we get there, okay?"

"Lana?"

"Hmm?"

"Thank you."

She blew him a kiss. "Welcome."

He began to drive, comforted by the sound of her breathing. She slipped into a doze, eventually sliding completely into sleep.

He understood now why Becketts withered and died when their mates did.

It had been two days, and already he couldn't imagine living without her.

Now he just had to get her to understand she could live with him.

Chapter Eleven

The next morning Lana woke to find herself in Chris's arms again. He'd tugged and prodded until she'd sleepily agreed to follow him upstairs. She hadn't been awake enough to realize he'd led her straight into his bedroom, and now here she was with her own warm werewolf at her back.

Frankly, saying anything about it at this point was probably stupid. The man had already had the milk, after all. No sense in complaining about the fact he'd stolen the cow and was getting set to raid the barn and move into the house.

"Chris."

His arm tightened slightly around her waist. He mumbled something incoherent.

She poked at his arm with her finger. It barely gave, the flesh tight over corded muscle. "Chris."

"Sleepin'."

"I noticed. But I need to get up."

"Nuh-uh. Sleepin'." He buried his face in her hair.

She'd only woken up with him twice and already she could see a pattern emerging. "It's morning."

"It's dark."

"How can you tell it's dark if you're sleeping?"

He sighed roughly. "Because I opened my eyes long enough

to look."

She patted his arm. "You have to let me up. I need to get ready for work."

"Can you get a job where you don't need to be up at o'dark hundred?"

She could hear both man and wolf whining in his voice. She was having a hard time holding back her smile. He sounded like a little boy whose favorite toy was being taken away. "I like my job, thank you."

He sighed. "I guess that means I have to be up too." He rolled over, pulling her on top of him. Once again she realized she was naked. It was hard to miss when his hardening cock was nudging her opening. "Geez, you're a demanding wench."

"Excuse mmph?" Her reply was lost when he pulled her down, kissing her like a starving man. Her traitorous body responded, bucking with a squeal when he slapped his hand against her ass. She reared up, breaking the kiss, startled at the feral look in his eyes. "Chris?"

His gaze drifted over her, the possession in it more of a turn-on than anything she'd ever experienced before. "I want you on your hands and knees."

She licked her lips, her body trembling at the command. The expression on his face, a feral need directed solely at her, would have been terrifying on another man.

On him it was hotter than hell.

She bent, and turned, and presented her ass to him, straddling his body. His cock was at her lips, bobbing gently, the tip glistening with pre-come.

"Suck it."

She leaned down and licked the drop, tasting the salty sweetness, savoring the flavor. She took the head into her

124

mouth, her head bobbing gently, more and more of him slipping between her lips until her nose was buried in the wiry curls at the base of his cock.

His knees bent, his hands stroking over her ass. "Eat my cock, little witch." He smacked the globe of her ass, making her moan around the hot flesh in her mouth. "Suck it until I tell you to stop."

She dragged her mouth up his cock, stopping long enough to lash the head with her tongue before once again taking him to the root.

"That's it, Lana." He smacked her ass again, making her tremble. "You like it, little witch?"

She didn't respond, too busy loving his cock.

He gently thrust up, showing her the rhythm he wanted. Every now and then a smack would land on her ass, making her shake and quiver.

No one had ever spanked her before, not like this. The urge to beg him to take her was beginning to override the need to taste his come.

"You want me to fuck you, Lana? You want me inside you?"

She was nodding before he'd finished, sucking extra hard on the head of his cock.

"Fuck! Stop, Lana!" His hand landed one more time on her ass. "Move to the edge of the bed and grab the footboard. Whatever you do, do not let go. You hear me?"

She nodded weakly, making her way to the foot of the bed. She was so ready for him she was trembling.

She felt him get to his knees behind her and grabbed the footboard blindly. "You want this?" The head of his cock stroked between her pussy lips. "Say you want this, Lana."

"Fuck me, Chris."

The head slipped in, stretching her. "Don't move those hands." His body bowed over hers, his cock settling into her, his hands coming to rest next to hers. His face was buried in the crook of her neck. She had the feeling she'd have another mark before they were done.

And then he began moving, and there was nothing gentle about it. It was a raw fucking, taking and taking her over and over again, the slap of his hips against her sore ass making her buck into him. She wanted this, wanted his passion, his need for her overriding everything else.

His knuckles were white. "Such a good little cocksucker." He shifted his knees, changing the angle, and there it was, that spot inside her getting expertly stroked, making her pussy weep with joy. "Gonna fuck you so good."

She began fucking back, thrusting into him, praying he would move faster. She groaned in approval when he picked up speed. "Wanna come?"

She nodded, too breathless to speak.

One large hand left the footboard, drifting over her breasts and down her stomach until his fingers grazed her clit. "Come for me."

He stroked her, his balls slapping against her wetness, his cock practically setting her pussy on fire. With a low, throaty groan she came, her back arching, her muscles quivering, stars dancing behind her eyes.

He pounded into her once, twice, and then he was coming too, moaning her name in her hair.

Lana let go of the footboard. Her entire body slumped, sated beyond belief.

He had to be the absolute best fuck she'd ever had. That he'd spanked her should have fazed her a bit, but the thought her wolfman liked his sex rough once in a while didn't bother

her at all. In fact, she'd gotten off on it big time. *We'll have to explore it more later. Much later. After I recover from this time.*

He curled up around her, almost purring with contentment. "Finding you has got to be the best thing that's ever happened to me."

She smiled, the soft kisses he peppered her neck with sending a shivery feeling down her spine. "Chris?"

"Hmm?"

"I have to go to work."

"Call. Out."

"No."

"Lana," he whined.

She tried to pull out of his arms. "This is what you get for liking morning sex. Nighttime sex we have time to cuddle. Morning sex and I have to log in to work."

"Aw, man." He let her go, waiting until she stood to right himself on the bed. He grabbed her pillow and burrowed into it. "Make coffee. Please?"

"Sure thing, wolfman." She reached down and kissed his cheek. "Go back to sleep, Chris."

"Mm-hmm." He snuggled down and was soon breathing softly, his big body relaxed into the bed. She took a moment to study him when he couldn't see it, couldn't comment on it. Broad, muscular shoulders covered in sleek, golden skin, dipped down temptingly into a narrow waist barely covered by the sheet.

She stared at the sheet for a moment, but couldn't help herself. She lifted the edge of it. God, he was so beautiful she still couldn't believe he wanted *her*. Her fingers were itching to do some walking over the tempting man-flesh, but she couldn't do it. She had to go to fucking *work*.

Soon? her libido whined. *Please? Pretty please with a cherry on top?*

Lana settled the blanket around his waist and tiptoed into the bathroom. Shutting the door, she banged her forehead against it repeatedly. A vision of him covered in whipped cream tried to take root in her brain. If she didn't get it out she'd crawl back into bed and take severe advantage of his naked hospitality. *Again.* At this rate her pussy would be fucked raw before the weekend!

"Lana? You okay?"

His sleepy, rumbly voice had her insides quivering. The concern she heard threatened to melt her heart. "Yeah, I'm fine. Just…banged something."

There was a pause. "Oh. You sure?"

Damn it, he has to be sweet too. "I'm sure."

"M'kay."

"Go to sleep, Chris."

"Mm."

She turned on the taps and grabbed her toothbrush. It wasn't until she was spitting the toothpaste down the sink that she even realized it *was* her toothbrush.

She tiptoed out of the bathroom and headed for the closet. There, her clothes hung neatly side by side with his. Her shoes lined the floor, her underwear sharing drawer space with his.

She couldn't even be upset about it. He'd obviously done this late last night after he'd gotten back from his run with Gareth. She'd been so tired she'd barely heard him coming into the room. He had to have been even more tired than she'd been, yet he'd still taken the time to carefully hang her clothing. He was such a *considerate* naked man.

She bit her lip, her gaze once more drawn to his sheet

covered form. *I wonder if I could really bounce a quarter off his glutes?*

She shook her head and grabbed the first thing her hand landed on, a pretty little sundress she liked to wear when visiting clients. She threw on her underwear and the dress, trying to ignore the little voice in her head wondering what Chris would think of it. She headed into the bathroom to find her makeup, figuring it was the most likely place Chris would put it.

Yup, he'd neatly placed her makeup kit right at the second sink. She quickly applied some makeup, brushed her hair, and headed down the stairs.

He might be able to sleep in, but some people around here needed to get to work by eight.

"Good morning, dear."

Lana stepped into the kitchen, smiling at the sweet scents drifting from the oven. "Good morning, Grammy. Umm, something smells good. What's for breakfast?"

Grammy pulled a tray out of the oven. "Honey buns."

Lana paused, the mug halfway to her lips. "Honey buns."

"Yes. What's the matter, dear? Usually you love honey buns."

Oh yeah. I adore *honey buns, especially the ones upstairs.* She could just picture them, covered in drizzled goodness, her teeth nipping at the firm, round globes. "Sounds good." She took a sip of her coffee, hoping she wasn't turning beet red. The heat she could feel in her cheeks, however, told her she probably was.

"Hmm." The buns landed on the stove quietly. "Why don't you get some plates for the buns?"

Lana held back her whimper and got the plate. *It's going to be a long day.*

She went ahead and set up her laptop in Chris's great room, nodding to him when he stumbled down the stairs. She watched him head into the kitchen, heard the coffee being poured, and then the rustle of the paper, his mumbled good morning to Annabelle barely audible. She smiled to herself, knowing he was checking out his teams. She wondered if he had to read the section more than once before the caffeine kicked in, or if it somehow trickled through his early morning decaffeinated fog.

About twenty minutes later, Chris walked in, cradling his mug. "Why are you on the floor?"

"I'm working." She entered another set of numbers, her eyes glued to the screen.

"Oh." She barely noticed him walking out.

She definitely noticed him walking back in, especially when he unplugged her laptop and picked it up. "Hey!"

He turned and walked out of the great room. Grabbing her mug, she scrambled to her feet and followed him. He set her computer down on his desk with a satisfied nod, plugging it in to the same surge protector his computer was on. "Better." Then he walked around the desk and settled into his chair. "Have a seat."

She glared at him. "You couldn't ask me if I wanted to move?"

"It's simple, really. Chair or floor? Nice dress, by the way."

"Thank you. What if I wanted floor?"

He looked at her over the reading glasses he'd slipped on. "Be my guest, but there's no coffee table in here. You might get uncomfortable." His smile was wolfish. "But if you really want to sit on the floor, just put the laptop between your legs and work that way. Oh, and make sure you sit—" he looked around and pointed, "—right there."

He'd picked a spot where he'd be able to look straight up her dress. If it wasn't for the teasing smile lurking around his mouth, she'd be pissed. "I liked you better before you found the coffee." She parked herself in the chair across from his desk, placing her mug on the coaster he handed her.

"Any musical preferences this morning?"

She sighed. "Something cheerful, please."

"Cheerful it is."

She pulled up the next set of figures she needed to work on, slowly losing track of the man across the desk. It wasn't until she'd finally entered the last of the numbers she realized what had been bothering her about the music he'd put on. "They Might Be Giants?"

He blinked, pulled from his own work, his eyes barely focused. "Build a little birdhouse in your soul."

She snorted delicately. "More like a doghouse."

"Why would I be in the doghouse?"

"How did I wind up naked in your bed *again?*"

"Sleeping with your clothes on makes you rumpled. Rumpled makes you uncomfortable. Therefore you needed to sleep without clothes." The innocent act he was trying to pull was completely ruined by the sexy grin lurking around the corners of his mouth.

"Really?" She folded her arms across her chest and glared at him.

He tried to look offended. "It's not like I broke out the webcam at any point during your semi or total nakedness, you know."

"Did I hear the word naked?" Gareth sauntered in, a can of soda in one hand and a smirk on his face. He settled on the edge of Chris's desk, looking back and forth at them. "Well?"

Chris was scowling at Gareth. "Lana's naked is no concern of yours."

"I know where you keep your webcam." Gareth took a sip of his soda and watched Chris.

Chris looked over at Lana. "Remind me to hide it. Last thing I want is us plastered all over some porno website."

"That's because you're a *good* dog, unlike some people who may need a trip to the p-o-u-n-d." She'd leaned forward, whispering the spelled word, hiding her mouth from Gareth and waggling her brows.

"So I guess you don't want to know I just heard back from the high council?"

Chris's head whipped around so fast Lana was surprised he didn't hurt himself. "And?"

"The king is considering a Beckett, all right." Gareth bent closer. "But it's not you."

The relief on Chris's face was wonderful to see. Lana had no desire to be the next wizard queen. "Thank the Gods. Any idea who he has in mind?"

Gareth shook his head. "They wouldn't say, but when I explained what was going on, they assured me you weren't the one. However, they *did* confirm Cole as originally the Godwin. They're going to let the king know what's going on. Odds are good he won't be in the running for long."

"Crap." Chris rubbed wearily at his face, settling his glasses back on his nose when he was done. "This isn't over. If the king dies before withdrawing Cole's name, he could have a legitimate claim to the throne."

"Nope, not over by a long shot." Gareth looked more serious than ever. "I think it's time to call in the cavalry."

Chris shivered. "Not yet."

"Who's the cavalry?" Lana saved her work and shut down for the day, logging out of her company's servers.

"Our brothers."

"Brothers? Huh. I thought you only had Daniel." She sat back with a grimace. The chair wasn't the most comfortable one in the world, and hunching forward to work on the laptop for the second day in a row had her back calling her all sorts of filthy names.

Chris frowned. "Why would you think that?"

"The Registry was really vague and kind of weird on... Sorry, I don't remember his name."

"Zach?" Chris rocked in his chair. The brothers exchanged a look. "Huh. I'll have to take a look and see what it says. Either way, Gareth's right. We need to call them in."

"Why? Wouldn't that put them in the line of fire too?"

Gareth stood and walked to the window. "I think it's time. They need to be aware of what's going on, and we definitely need to...tell... Guys?" There was an odd tone in Gareth's voice. He stared out the window, horror growing on his face.

"What?" Christopher stood, the look on his brother's face pushing him to his brother's side.

Gareth pointed. "Look outside."

Lana joined them by the window to see what Gareth was looking at. Chris was stunned, the sight of what was rolling towards them leaving him speechless.

"Holy fuck." Lana leaned forward, wide-eyed at the huge bank of storm clouds racing in their direction. Lightning arched from cloud to cloud in a dazzling, lethal display. The clouds were a sickly greenish gray. "That's no ordinary storm."

The brothers exchanged glances. "It's Cole." Christopher pulled Lana to him protectively, tucking her under his arm. "We need to stop it before an innocent gets hurt."

Gareth started to disrobe, much to Lana's obvious delight. Christopher turned her and blocked her view of his almost naked brother. "Open the window. I'll go scout and see what I can find out. Maybe he's holed up nearby."

Christopher opened the window in time for Gareth, now in wolf form, to leap through. He landed on the ground a story below and took off with a brief bark up at them.

"Whoa."

He couldn't help himself. He slapped Lana on the ass. "What were you doing looking?"

She rubbed her ass. "Hello! Hunk getting some naked time. You expected me *not* to look?"

"When we have a few free hours we're going to have to explore this whole concept of *naked time*." He strode for the door. "Make yourself at home. I'll be in my workroom trying to figure out what the hell Cole is up to."

"I might be able to help."

He smiled back at her. "Wizard and witch, remember, sweetheart?" He frowned. He couldn't keep doing that to her. She'd more than proved herself, no matter how much he wanted her to stay out of it. "No. I know you held off the wolf in the car. If you want to try and work it out on your own, feel free. But without knowing Cole, you'll be at a serious disadvantage." He couldn't protect her while he tried to unravel the storm, but he knew someone who could. "If you're really planning on trying something, see if Annabelle can help." When he'd last seen

Annabelle she'd been attempting to scry once more on Cole, but she'd drop it in a heartbeat if she thought Alannah was in any danger.

Lana's grin looked almost evil. "Oh, I think I can come up with something to brighten Cole's day."

He strode over to her and chucked her under the chin. He was worried. What if she tried something when he wasn't there to protect her and Cole's protections lashed out? *Maybe encouraging her isn't such a good idea.* "Stay out of trouble."

She blinked up at him, all sweet innocence. "Trouble? *Moi?*"

He couldn't keep the slow smile off his face. "You're going to drive me insane, aren't you?" He didn't let her answer, just took advantage of her open lips to lay siege to her mouth.

She was absolutely delicious. He would never get enough of her taste. He threaded his fingers through her thick hair, holding her in place while he slowly devoured her mouth. After only a moment's hesitation, her lips joined his in the dance, moving against his own in a shy exploration that had him weak in the knees and rock hard in seconds. He realized he'd never tire of the sweet moans pouring from her mouth. The fact that her kisses were still shy after the incredible sex they'd been having was, to his mind, a good thing. It meant she was taking it, taking *them*, seriously.

Lightning lit the room, followed by the booming crash of thunder. Christopher pulled back, allowing himself to linger for just a moment. He stared down at her, amazed at how quickly his little witch had wormed her way into his heart. From the dazed look on her face, perhaps she was finally starting to see him as something more than a wizard too. Maybe she was finally seeing him as a man.

It was going to be a pain doing spell work with a hard-on, but if Cole's games were going to be stopped, he'd have to get to work. "Stay inside where it's safe, sweetheart. Please. I don't want you outside where Cole could find you."

He waited for her to nod, but was forced to accept her shrug. Vaguely dissatisfied, he headed to his workroom to try and untangle the knotted roots of Cole's storm, hoping Lana was smart enough to stay safe.

Chapter Twelve

"Chris?"

"Hmm?"

"Can I borrow some feathers?"

He blinked, looking up from his big old book in the middle of the table. Cute glasses were perched on the end of his nose. He looked incredibly intelligent and sexy, like one of those hunky college professors girls dreamed of getting and never actually did. Those glasses were probably going to be the final nail in her denial's coffin. "Feathers?"

"Mm-hmm. White, blue, yellow and black."

"All on one feather or one of each?"

"One of each."

He reached into a cupboard behind him and pulled out the feathers she asked for.

"Thanks!" She took the feathers, planted a kiss on his cheek, and hustled out of his workroom, knowing he was shaking his head at her.

Lana had already ransacked his cupboards and pantry for the other ingredients she needed. The feathers had been the last bit. He'd even had the black rope she needed in his bedroom. And if he'd used it for what she thought he'd used it for, it was better going where she planned to send it.

If he wanted to play *those* kinds of games with her he could damn well buy new rope.

She ran out the back door and onto the patio, into the teeth of the storm, ignoring the fact that she'd been turned on at the thought of playing *those* kinds of games with Chris. *Just not with the rope he used with other women.* Not if *she* had anything to say about it.

She had to work fast. Lightning was beginning to strike all around the house, the flashes coming closer and closer together, forming a cage they might not be able to break free from. If Chris or Annabelle caught her out here she'd never hear the end of it. She just knew what she had planned would work, but she needed the time to *make* it work.

She took the large glass mixing bowl and put the feathers inside. Holding them down with one hand she began to pour salt over the feathers. The salt was meant to ground the wind, represented by the feathers.

At first she wasn't certain it was working, but she persevered. She visualized the winds dying down gradually, and it began to work. When the last feather was covered the winds had died down until only a light, natural breeze remained. The lightning stopped, but the tang of ozone was still in the air.

Nodding in satisfaction, she took two wooden mixing spoons and bound them together in the shape of an X. She set the X on the wet ground just off the concrete patio and began pouring the salt over it.

"Evil storm that rides the sky,

It is time for you to fly.

Lord and Lady hear my plea.

As I will so mote it be."

The rain stopped. There was a sense of expectation to the

air, like the lightning was poised to strike again at any moment. If it did, her spell would be undone.

Damn, Cole is strong. The storm should have been wiped out, but some force behind it was keeping it in place. *Better work fast.* She pulled out the black rope, carefully cut down to thirteen inches, and began tying it in knots. With each one she chanted, pouring her power into each knot until her hands were shaking with fatigue. If this didn't work, the storm would return in full force.

"Knot of one my spell begun.

Knot of two my words are true.

Knot of three it comes to be.

Knot of four the storm is no more.

Knot of five this spell is alive.

Knot of six my protection fix.

Knot of seven, power is given.

Knot of eight protect my mate.

Knot of nine completes my rhyme."

With a satisfied smile she saw the clouds begin to break up. She took the spoons and the rope, wrapped them in some white cheesecloth and began digging in the dirt.

"What the fuck do you think you're doing?"

She ignored Chris's irate voice in favor of burying the spoons and knots. If she didn't hurry, the spell could still be undone. She could feel Cole's power testing the knots, trying to pull the storm free of the binding spell. The binding needed the grounding of the earth to hold it in place. Without it, her knots could be unraveled, and she'd have to start all over again, and she was already exhausted.

"Cole's storm packed one hell of a punch," she muttered, patting the wet soil down over the spell with a final surge of power. Now nothing could get to it. She sat back on her heels, closing her eyes and lifting her face to the sky. The cool wet air wafted over her face, soothing now without the wizard fury behind it.

"You should have let me deal with it."

She found herself lifted off the ground, not that she cared. Her legs were shaking so badly she wasn't certain they would hold her up.

"Sorry, Chris. There was something about the storm, something not right. It needed to be gone."

He sighed. "This is why you can't deal with Cole, sweetheart."

"Mmm?" Man, she couldn't remember the last time spell work had tired her out so much. It usually left her feeling like she needed a good nap, but this? She felt like she could sleep for a week.

"I told you before. Wizards do things slowly, in stages, needing only one small component at the end of the spell to activate it. We usually have several charms on our person at any given time, only needing the right words to activate the spells. Witches do everything at once, in one big bang. No way could you take on the multiple spells Cole would be casting. Remember how tired you were from the spell you did in the car?"

She opened one bleary eye and stared up at him. His expression was full of annoyed concern. "'Kay."

One dark brow rose in disbelief. "Really? Not going to argue with me anymore on that?"

She burrowed closer to his chest. "Sleepy. Don't wanna argue."

He sighed and settled her down on something soft. *Bed,* her tired brain registered. "It was a very powerful storm. No wonder you're a tired little witch." She felt him remove her shoes. "Sleep, sweetheart. I'll take care of you."

"'Kay." She struggled through the thick layers of tired to reach for him. "Chris?"

"Hmm?"

"Night."

She felt his lips brush hers before falling back through those layers and into the arms of Morpheus.

"Your little witch is extremely powerful, Christopher."

"Yes, she is." Christopher sipped at his tea, staring at the roaring fire. Lana had slept through dinner. He didn't expect her to wake until morning, and that was fine with him. At least he knew what she was up to. Part of him was furious at her for putting herself in danger; the other part was furious with himself for not realizing what she'd been up to. "It's a good thing I felt her spell taking hold. I'd already started to cast mine. Things might have gotten...interesting if they'd clashed."

"Drought for certain, not sure what else." Gareth stretched. "Why don't you go for a run? I'll keep an eye on your little witch, keep her safe."

"From *outside* the bedroom?" Christopher mock-glared at his brother. He knew Gareth would lay down his life for Lana. It was the Beckett way, and whether she wanted to admit it or not, Lana was most definitely a Beckett.

Gareth laughed. "From outside the bedroom." He laid a hand on Christopher's shoulder. "Go on. Your wolf must be getting restless. I've already had my run."

Christopher nodded. His wolf was dying to get outdoors,

but they were both leery of leaving their mate unprotected in their den while there was an enemy nearby. Christopher knew he could trust his big brother. Gareth would have to be dead for Cole to get one finger near Lana at this point.

He stood and headed to the patio. "I'll be back in a bit."

"Take your time, bro. I'm not going anywhere."

He shot his brother a grin on his way out the door. "Gareth? Thanks."

Gareth nodded, looking determined. "Becketts stick together."

He shifted, taking joy in the night air and the knowledge his mate was safely inside, sleeping in his bed.

"Becketts stick together."

He was halfway into the woods before he realized what *that* meant.

Shit. Gareth had already called in the cavalry. He wondered when they would arrive and if he'd have time to warn Lana about the bevy of Becketts about to descend on them.

Chapter Thirteen

Christopher got back from his run to find all three of his brothers waiting for him.

"Any problems?" Gareth held out his pants with a smirk.

He shifted to human once more, used to being naked in front of his brothers. "Nope." He'd been surprised to find the run uneventful. He had to smile at the thought that the unraveling of Cole's spell had left the other wizard too tired to pull any further crap for the night. And it was all thanks to his little witch.

Still, he'd been hoping he'd been wrong and his brothers wouldn't be here quite so soon. It was bad enough he had to share space with Gareth. Daniel and Zachary weren't going to be leaving any time soon. "You had to call them, didn't you?"

Zachary, the youngest, tossed a peanut M&M up in the air, catching it with his mouth. "Heard you had some problems."

Daniel, the next youngest, caught Zach's next candy and popped it in his own mouth. "From what Gareth said you could use some help."

Zach shoved Daniel. "Hey! That was mine, asshole."

"You're the one who threw a perfectly good M&M." Daniel smirked.

Christopher finished dressing, still glaring at Gareth.

"Remind me again why we need them?"

Zachary grinned. "Dude, one Beckett has problems, all the Becketts have...*hello*." Zachary stopped, his expression turning wicked, his eyes glued to the doorway into the great room.

Christopher turned, knowing what Zachary was staring at with such fascination. Lana stood in the doorway, looking startled and deliciously rumpled. She was wearing one of his shirts. Thank the Gods it hung low on her thighs or he'd be forced to pluck his brothers' eyeballs out. "What are you doing out of bed?"

"A, I'm an adult, I can get out of bed in the middle of the night. B, I was thirsty." She pointed a thumb at his brothers. "When did the rest of the litter get here?"

Daniel's brows rose into his hair. "Litter?"

Christopher walked over to Lana, ignoring Gareth's chuckles, and pulled her into a light hold. "Lana, I'd like you to meet my brothers." He pointed to Zachary, the only one of the brothers whose eyes weren't gold. They were a soft misty blue, and chock full of mischief. "Zachary Beckett, the youngest."

Zachary leaned in and kissed her cheek. "Pleased to meet you."

"Daniel, the next youngest."

Daniel merely nodded, but his serious gaze never left Lana's face.

Lana yawned. "Nice to meet you." She turned in Christopher's embrace. "You're out of milk."

He blinked. "Since when? I bought a quart yesterday morning."

"And this evening I finished it." She bit her lip. "Sorry."

"Don't be. I'll send one of the boys out for more." He kissed the tip of her nose. "Anything else you need?"

144

"More milk?"

He smiled down at her. "I'll make sure you have some for breakfast. Go on back to bed, you look exhausted." When she frowned, he decided to play dirty. "Please, sweetheart. If you're going to help me figure out how to deal with Cole, I need you well rested."

She made a cute little face before pulling out of his arms. He was gratified to see the reluctance. "All right. But only because you asked so nicely." She smiled up at him. "Good night, Chris." She peeked around him and waved languidly, tipping her head and yawning so wide he thought he could see straight to her feet. "Good night, Beckett pups."

Gareth grinned, Zachary laughed outright, and Daniel just shook his head.

Chris kept an eye on her until he saw her start up the stairs, then turned to face his brothers with a warning growl. "Paws off my mate, Zachary."

"Yeah, yeah." Zachary waved him off, his expression sobering. "She can't fight Cole, Chris."

"I know, but she seems to think otherwise."

"Your mate's a witch." Daniel was studying him, his expression revealing nothing.

Christopher tensed. He hadn't thought his brothers would have taken issue with the fact that his mate wasn't a wizard, but if they did, they'd have to get over it. "Yes, she is. Is there a problem?"

Daniel smiled. "Not on my end."

"Not on mine, either." Zachary picked up another peanut M&M and tossed it into the air, his face relaxing once more into its usual devil-may-care expression.

Daniel caught it. "Does she know what we are?" He fended

off Zachary's attempt to get the M&M back.

Christopher grinned. "Yes. She does. She had more problems with the fact I'm a wizard than she did with the wolf."

Daniel and Zachary stopped fighting over the M&M. "Seriously?" Zachary let go of Daniel's fist and lightly punched Christopher in the shoulder. "Congrats, bro!"

Daniel took advantage of Zachary's distraction to pop the candy into his mouth. "Congratulations."

Gareth stood up from where he'd been lounging against the patio table. "This calls for a celebration."

"No, it doesn't." Christopher got between his brothers and his kitchen. "The last time you celebrated in my house my cleaning lady quit without notice."

"Is it our fault she walked in while we were changing?" Zachary shrugged and walked around Christopher into the kitchen, heading straight for the fridge. For a man with the build of a runner he packed an awful lot of food into his lean frame.

"You should have warned us she was coming in that day." Daniel shook his head. "We would have gotten back sooner and at least had our pants on."

"Instead she got an eyeful of naked ass." Gareth sniggered. "In more ways than one."

Zach snarled at Gareth. "Dickhead. Three minutes sooner and she would have gotten the shock of her life. Hey, you got any cheddar?"

Christopher groaned, watching both Daniel and Zachary empty his fridge, his fears confirmed. Daniel and Zachary had no intention of leaving any time soon. "No, I don't."

"Damn it. It's my favorite, especially with grapes."

"Go buy some. Bring back milk while you're out."

Zachary grumbled, but pulled out his car keys.

"Beer run?" Daniel joined Zachary, heading toward the front door.

Zachary made a face. "Nah, wine for me."

The two headed out, leaving Christopher and Gareth alone in the kitchen. "Help me put this stuff away."

Gareth sighed and began repacking the fridge. "Think they'll return by morning?"

Christopher just glared at his brother and put the grapes back in the crisper.

She was still sleeping when he entered his bedroom later that night. He watched her, unable to stop himself from stroking her hair away from her cheek. He loved it when she was sleeping; her face was so soft and innocent...

He frowned. She was cold, and pale. He leaned closer, dread filling him.

She was barely breathing.

"Fuck." Hopping from the bed, he ran for the door. "Gareth! Annabelle!"

Doors slammed open, feet came running, and soon all of the Becketts, plus Annabelle, were in his bedroom. When Zach and Daniel had returned from their run he had no clue, but he was grateful they were there. He was doubly grateful his brothers were dressed. "Something's wrong with Lana."

Annabelle rushed to the bed. "Let me see." She placed her hand on her granddaughter's cheek, pulling it back with a startled look. "She's cold as ice!"

"We need to warm her." He picked Lana up and tried to ignore the way her breath was beginning to stutter in her chest.

"Zach, start the water. Daniel, get a warming charm on that blanket. Gareth, I need you to put another protection spell on the room. Somehow Cole got through mine." He had no doubt who had tried to harm his mate. But how had he done it? He'd never laid a hand on her, so sympathetic magic, like he'd used with the wolf hairs, wasn't an option.

Zach preceded him into the bathroom, muttering under his breath, so low Christopher couldn't make out the words. He turned on the water and began filling the tub once it was hot enough to suit Christopher.

Annabelle stood in the doorway and watched, worried. "We need to take the hex off of her."

Christopher turned and stared at her. "Hex?" Cole couldn't do hexes; only warlocks did hexes. Cole was most definitely a wizard. Besides, a hex most definitely required something of the victim's to bind the magic.

Oh fuck. Her damn car was still out on the road. Cole could have pulled something from it.

Hell. Cole could do something to Lana whenever he wanted.

Fuck!

Annabelle nodded. "If that isn't a hex I don't know what one is."

"Damn." There could be only one explanation. Cole had help. *Warlock* help. "Is the tub full yet?"

Zach was mumbling under his breath, stirring the water with...bath oils?

"Zach?"

"Almost ready." He frowned, his face determined and vaguely un-Zach-like. His little brother *never* looked this serious. "I need a white candle."

Christopher opened his mouth to object but before he

could, Annabelle turned. "Be right back."

"What do you need the white candle for?"

Zach looked toward the bath. "The uncrossing."

Christopher blinked. "Uncrossing." He shifted Lana's cool body in his arms. "Care to explain?"

Zach looked up at him. Something in his younger brother's eyes scared him. He'd never been scared of Zach before. Zach had less power than almost any other wizard he knew, so little he was barely a blip in The Registry. So why did the expression on his little brother's face bother him so much? "I need the white candle, Chris."

"Here." Annabelle handed it over.

Zach examined it and made an impatient noise. He pulled out his penknife and carved something into the white surface.

"What are you doing?"

Annabelle's confusion now matched Christopher's own. What *was* Zach doing?

Zach finished carving the candle. Christopher got a good look at the symbol and nearly swallowed his tongue.

Zach had carved a symbol that had Christopher's heart jumping. Three hammer-like arms were drawn equidistant from one another in a triskelion-like design without lifting the knife from the wax. In the center of the symbol was a wheeling sun, the six rays bent back as if in a wind. The maze-like drawing was then surrounded by a perfect circle. It was a symbol rarely seen, since there were those who considered this particular aspect of the Goddess to be on the dark side. "Hecate's wheel? Zach, what the fuck?"

"Trust me." Zach picked up yet another oil and rubbed it on the candle. The room smelled woodsy, each of the oils complementary in their scents. Christopher could detect juniper, rosemary and the bitter scent of rue.

Rue? Where did he get rue *oil?* Chris didn't think he had any rue oil in his den. He certainly didn't have it in his bathroom, considering its best use was for removing curses.

Chris looked at Annabelle, who shrugged. "Trust him."

She looked as baffled as he felt. "Fine. Let's get her in the bath." Zach lit the candle and held it while Christopher lowered Lana into the tub, still wearing her nightgown. He'd take it off of her once his brothers were out of the room.

Once he could reassure himself she was safe.

He held her head above the water, debating whether or not to send Gareth to his workroom. One or two other things there might be useful in breaking a hex.

"Chris?"

He closed his eyes, going through his inventory. Now that the bath water was warming her up he could have Zach hold her steady while he checked his cabinets.

"Chris? She's not blue anymore."

He opened his eyes. Lana was stirring, frowning, and her lips were pink once more. Her arm splashed, her wet hand pushing her hair away from her forehead. "What the hell?" Her teeth were clacking together so hard he was afraid she'd chip a tooth or bite her tongue.

Chris nearly passed out from the relief. "Goddess, Lana, you scared me." He pulled her to him, reveling in the feel of her warming skin.

"Um, okay? What did I do?" The chattering of her teeth was slowing down, the chill in her skin almost completely gone.

He kissed her, keeping it light and quick. "You were hexed."

She sat up, looking startled. "Hexed?"

"Yes."

She scowled. "Let me up." When he tried to protest, because really, he thought he could still detect a hint of coolness to her skin, she barked, *"Now."*

Zach put the candle down and grabbed a towel. "Yes, ma'am."

She stepped, dripping, from the tub. "How could Cole hex me? He's a wizard."

"He has to have a warlock helping him. It's the only logical explanation." Christopher wrapped her in the towel, picked her up and carried her into the bedroom.

Annabelle followed, her gaze glued to Lana's face. "How are you feeling, dear?" She glanced at the bathroom and looked startled, but turned back to Lana with a strained smile.

Gareth was walking around the room, incense burning in a censer he carried. He was muttering a simple but powerful charm. "Lord and Lady, hear my plea. Protect us from adversity."

"Fine, Grammy." Lana settled on the pillows, taking Christopher's hand and recapturing his attention. Her own hand was shaking. "What happened?"

Christopher shuddered. "I came into the room, and you were ice cold and barely breathing."

"Yeah, sounds like a hex all right." She wriggled under the comforter, finally throwing the soaking wet nightgown onto the floor with a sigh. "What is the man thinking?"

"That his tame warlock will get the entire karmic backlash." Zach entered the room and settled onto the bed next to Christopher. He looked weary. Darks circles had appeared under his eyes and the corners of his mouth were pinched and drawn. "Otherwise I don't think even he would be willing to go to these extremes."

"Room's protected." Gareth put the censer down on Christopher's bureau. "Anything else we can do to help?"

Christopher eyed the wet nightgown on the floor. He had a powerful urge to see how naked Lana was under the covers. "Yup. Out. Thanks."

Zach chuckled. "Sure thing, bro." He stood and clapped Christopher on the shoulder. "See you in the morning."

Christopher watched his baby brother leave the room with a thoughtful frown. Zach had done something in the bath he hadn't expected from such a weak wizard. He'd broken a hex powerful enough to kill. And from the look on Annabelle's face, she'd have some words of her own for him.

What the hell was going on?

"You sure you feel okay?" Gareth stood over Lana and touched her arm. Chris had to fight the urge to rip Gareth's hand off. The knowledge that his mate had nearly died and was now naked under those covers was making his wolf very territorial. If it had been anyone but one of his brothers, he might not have even thought about stopping. He'd be holding a bloody body part.

"I'm fine, Papa Bear. I'll have Chris bring me a glass of water and everything."

Gareth shook his head. "Then I'll leave the two of you alone. Get some sleep." He poked Chris on the shoulder. "I mean it. She's still tired from the spellcasting, plus the effects of the hex. Sleep now, sex later."

Chris growled, but secretly he had to admit his brother was right. Dark circles ringed Lana's eyes even more darkly than they'd ringed Zach's. "Good night, Gareth."

Annabelle was the last to leave. She'd already picked up the wet nightgown and placed it in the hamper. "Well, I'll let you two get some rest. If you need me again just holler." She paused at the doorway, staring thoughtfully down the hallway. "I wonder if...?"

"What, Grammy?" Lana yawned.

Annabelle smiled at Lana. "Never mind. We'll discuss it later." She left the room, the remnants of her smile fading. She closed the door behind her, finally leaving them alone.

"I'm all right, Chris. Really." Lana yawned again, wide enough that he could practically see her feet. "Just tired."

"Get some sleep, little witch. I'm going to get undressed, then I'll join you." And really, he too was exhausted.

"M'kay." She curled up on her side. "G'night."

"Good night." He wasn't even certain she heard him. She was almost asleep already. He took off all his clothes and tossed them in the hamper on top of the wet nightgown. He headed into the bathroom to brush his teeth.

Zach's white candle was sitting on the countertop, the smell of rue oil still bitter in his nostrils. The Wheel of Hecate was now outlined in sickly green, the remnants of the hex curling around the never-ending maze, bleeding off before his eyes.

He picked up the candle, startled at the strength of Zach's lingering magic. Annabelle's curious words came back to him. *I wonder?*

Chapter Fourteen

Lana woke up the next morning feeling completely refreshed. The sun streaked in through the windows, warming her. Her bedroom window faced away from the rising sun so she just knew she'd overslept. She stretched, thinking about the day ahead. Thank the Lord and Lady her job allowed her to telecommute, otherwise she'd be in deep shit for sleeping so late.

She opened her eyes, smiling at the start of a new day.

A man with the most gorgeous pair of golden brown eyes smiled back.

Lana shrieked and almost fell out of the bed, but the man attached to the pretty eyes caught her.

"Good morning to you too." The man jiggled his finger in his ear with a grimace.

Chris. Right. She put her hand on her chest. Her breathing still wasn't back to normal. "Crap." Why hadn't she remembered Chris? She hadn't been *that* out of it, had she? "What time is it?"

"About nine o'clock." He stretched lazily, displaying an amazing amount of bronzed skin. The sheet dipped enticingly low. She had to resist the urge to help it along, the memory of the gorgeous body underneath taunting her. He rolled toward her and shrugged, the sheet dropping enough she could see his hip bones. "You were so tired I decided to let you sleep. If you want to be pissed about it, go ahead, but I did what I felt was right."

She nodded and tried to drag her libido into line, but the image of his naked body had bought a condo in her brain and moved in to stay. *Damn that sneaky morning sex. Tricky dog.* "What day is it?"

"Friday. Why?"

She winced. "Crap. Tomorrow's the wedding."

She bit her lip as Chris's entire body tensed. "Wedding."

"Um. Yes. Kelly Andrews and Dennis Littleton."

"Who? And why are these people worth your life?"

"Kelly and Kerry are twins, and two of my best friends. Dennis is...a nice guy?" She smiled at him hopefully, but was pretty sure this was one battle she wasn't going to win. "Wednesday's party was for Kelly. It was her bachelorette party, remember?"

"Who does a bachelorette party in the middle of the week?" Chris flopped against the pillows, his arms behind his head.

"It was supposed to be a surprise party, except the bride wasn't all that surprised. I think her twin spilled the beans."

He grunted, the frown on his face darkening, possibly thinking about the half-naked men she'd supposedly partied with the other night. She didn't dare tell him about the twenty bucks' worth of ones she'd shoved into some masculine g-strings. Her wolf would have a major hissy fit if he found out.

"Yup. Brides do this little thing called getting married. It usually happens on a Saturday or Sunday, depending on your religious preferences. Frankly, I'm partial to Friday nights myself. The rates are cheaper and the religious people are more available."

Chris was already shaking his head. "We can't go. It's too dangerous."

Lana sighed. "I don't think I have a choice. I'm a bridesmaid, and Kelly, the bride? She's mundane. I can't exactly call her and tell her I'm dropping out of her wedding due to a bad case of evilwizarditis."

Chris growled. "Well, you'll have to come up with some reason for dropping out, because your life is more important to me than a party, even a wedding."

"There's no way she can replace me last minute." She ignored the incredulous look he gave her, concentrating on how to get out of this particular little pickle. "Besides, I gave my word."

He closed his eyes. "You gave your word on what?"

"I'd be there to keep Kerry from pushing Dennis too far."

"Dennis is the groom?"

"Yup, and a man with a bigger stick up his rectum has never been found. Kerry loves yanking his stick too, and Kelly gets stuck in the middle."

"So you promised Kelly you'd stand in between Kerry and Dennis?"

"Not quite. I promised Kerry I would. See, Dennis makes Kelly happy, but drives Kerry nuts. She can't help herself, but she doesn't want to make Kelly upset on her wedding day. And I have to say Dennis is a good sport about it usually."

"Huh." He reached over and pulled Lana on top of him, thus proving once and for all that, yes, he definitely slept naked. She could feel his steely erection poking her thigh, distracting her from the wedding. "If Cole knows about your family he knows you'll be at the wedding tomorrow. You might as well wear a dress with concentric circles on it and yell 'shoot me now!'"

She thumped her head down on his bare chest with a groan. "What do I do? They'll never forgive me. I *have* to be there." She settled in, soothed by the sound of his heartbeat. "We have to make this work, Chris. It's important to me."

"All right, Lana. If it means that much to you, we'll work something out." He stroked her back, his tone thoughtful. "Remember what I said about how wizards work their magic?"

"Yes?"

"It's entirely possible he already has something in place for the wedding. Actually, it's highly probable he has something in place."

"Could it be something that will happen whether or not we show up?"

"Good question. If it's something triggered by our presence, then we need to avoid your friend's wedding like the plague. But if it's something meant to go off at a specific time and place, *regardless* of our presence..."

"They'd be sitting ducks. Two families of mundanes under magical attack." She grimaced. "Not even Cole would risk the karma backlash on something like that, tame warlock or not."

"His little thunderstorm didn't start right over us, sweetheart. Odds are good he's already hurt innocents." His fist clenched in her hair. "What the fuck is wrong with him? He has to know there's no way the king will name him his heir once he gets wind of this!"

"Unless he hopes the king will be so far gone by the time he does it won't matter anymore."

Chris frowned. "The council would act. There'd be a civil war, those loyal to the new king, those who oppose the very idea of how Cole was crowned. It would throw us into total chaos."

He gasped. "Could you not squirm, sweetheart? I'm *really* trying to be good here but all I want to do is fuck you until we both scream, and I figure we should wait until *after* we talk."

Lana froze.

"Damn." His laughing groan was rueful. "Me and my big mouth."

She closed her eyes. He wanted her, she wanted him, but damn it, they had too much to do! "Not this morning. Okay?"

She could feel every muscle in his body tense. "This afternoon?"

She looked down into his hopeful face. *Damn. Puppy dog eyes.* "We'll see."

He swiftly muttered a prayer of thanks before giving her a deep, hungry kiss that curled her fingers and toes. Her fingers weren't too upset about it, since they were currently curling into warm, hard man.

Which was why the slap on her ass was so surprising. She reared back with a yelp. "What was that for?"

"You need to move. You're late for work, and we have a wedding to prepare for."

"What about the danger?" She damn near swallowed her tongue when Chris got out of the bed and stretched, completely uncaring of his...*oh boy. Pretty.* Her fingers were itching to glide over all his smooth skin and drag him back into bed.

"Do you think Annabelle can keep my brothers in line?"

He walked toward the master bathroom, yawning. She tilted her head, enjoying the flex of his ass. "Hmm?" He turned. She suddenly found herself confronted by the most tempting bit of man flesh she'd ever seen. Not overly long, not too fat, it looked like mouthwatering perfection. The fact it belonged only to her was finally beginning to sink in.

His wicked chuckle dragged her gaze from his cock, now standing at full attention, to his face. "Can Annabelle keep my brothers in line?"

That arrogant male smirk of his was going to get him into a lot of trouble, she just knew it. "I think Annabelle could keep the US Marine Corps in line if she wanted to. Why?"

"Because between the four of us, plus your Grammy if she'll help, we should be able to keep your friends, and you, safe from whatever Cole has cooked up." He headed into the bathroom and started running water, probably to brush his teeth. "Besides, if we're pretty sure he's going to hit us at the wedding, it might be the perfect opportunity to lay a trap of our own."

Lana scrambled out of bed. "If Kerry and Kelly can be kept safe, I think it's a great idea."

He didn't answer, but that was all right. She had a few ideas of her own on how to keep her friends, and her family, safe the next day. For once she was going to do what Chris wanted without arguing.

She was calling out sick.

Christopher was startled at how Lana worked. Watching her work her magic was like watching an intricate dance, one he barely knew the steps to and couldn't keep up in. She flitted from item to item, throwing seemingly random things into a pot on the stove, sniffing it, pondering it, before adding something else to the mixture. Annabelle was mixing dried herbs and oils together into a potpourri smelling strongly of dried carnations and cedar. The two women chatted about the wedding, but something in the way they spoke let him know their chatter was somehow a part of what they were doing.

He was this close to ordering pizza for dinner, because he didn't think he'd get his kitchen back anytime soon.

Zach was watching everything with an intensity Chris wasn't used to seeing in him. He watched every move both Annabelle and Lana made, sometimes frowning, sometimes nodding, but mostly looking thunderstruck.

Chris snuck out of the kitchen. He had one more thing to double check. If he was right, it would be a shock to everyone in the family, but he doubted it would be a shock to Annabelle.

"Are they still in there?"

Chris snorted. "I think they're going to be in there for quite a while."

Daniel frowned. "What's Zach doing?"

"Watching them."

"Why?"

Chris almost answered him, but the casual contempt in Daniel's tone stopped him. Daniel needed to learn to leave Zach alone; he was the one most likely to pick on Zach thanks to Zach's apparent lack of power. And if Chris was right, Zach would soon be able to get some of his own back. "Do me a favor and order some pizzas, will you? I have some work to do."

"Sure thing. Move, Zach." Daniel pushed his brother away, ignoring Zach's growling response. "Pepperoni?"

Zach's verbal growling stopped, but his stomach piped up. "Sounds good."

"Oh, pizza? Can I have mushrooms and garlic and tomatoes?" Lana reached out for yet another dried herb, barely turning away from her pot.

"Got it." Daniel picked up the phone and prepared to make the call.

Chris touched Daniel's shoulder to get his attention. "Make

sure you pick the pizza up; don't have it delivered."

Daniel gave him a thumbs-up. "Pick-up, please."

Chris headed for his workroom and The Registry. *I wonder if I'm right, and Zach is a witch, not a wizard.*

Chapter Fifteen

Chris woke from the most wonderfully erotic dream he'd ever had to the feel of something wet and warm lapping at his cock. He stretched and smiled, knowing just what, or rather *who*, was going on. "Morning, little witch." He opened his eyes to the prettiest sight he'd ever seen. Lana's hair hung over her face, hiding what she was doing from him. He reached down and gently pulled her hair back, enjoying the sight of her swollen lips moving up and down his cock.

"Mmm." Her smile was sensuous, her eyes tangling with his, her expression hot and hungry. She lowered down and down until her nose brushed his pubic hair, and he damn near lost his mind.

"Shit, sweetheart. Do that again." She pulled off and slowly, oh so slowly, lowered herself down on him again. "God. Oh fuck. Tongue. Use your tongue." He watched, entranced, while she made love to him with her mouth. He longed to let go and fuck into her but he held back, terrified he'd hurt his beautiful mate.

She shot him a heated look and turned, presenting her ass and pretty pussy to him.

"Swing your leg over, sweetheart." She obeyed, and there it was, his favorite meal in the world, all spread out and ready for him to feast. With a growl, he tugged her down until he could taste her to his heart's content.

Her sweet mouth was about to drive him insane. He could barely concentrate on what he was doing to her, but from the moans he must have been doing it right.

He began nibbling on her clit, sucking it into his mouth and laving it with his tongue. Her groan felt incredible around his cock so he did it again, and again, until she was thrusting against his mouth. The suction on his cock increased until he thought she'd pull his brains out the tip, and right then and there he really didn't care if she did. He was so damn close to spilling down her throat, but he wanted her to go over the edge first.

Chris pulled off of her long enough to drench one of his fingers in her juices, making sure it was good and wet before pressing up against the pucker of her ass.

The suction on his cock paused, but he didn't. He sucked her clit into his mouth, earning him another mind-shattering groan around the crown of his cock. She bucked into him, fucking him, pressing the tip of his finger into her ass without thought.

She gasped, stilling. He waited, allowing her to get used to the feel of his finger there. If he had his way he'd eventually have his cock in the snug passage of her ass, preferably sooner rather than later. For now, he soothed her with laps of his tongue around her snug hole, fucking his tongue into her pussy and his finger into her ass. He used his free hand to thumb her clit, hoping the sensations would ease the burn he knew she felt when his finger stroked deeper.

He wished he had another set of hands. He wanted so desperately to grab hold of her head, push her down onto him, show her the rhythm he liked best. Instead he stroked her clit harder and was rewarded by a low hum of approval that nearly blew his head off. His hips jerked, shoving his cock farther into her mouth. She rewarded him by sucking him in deeper, stroking him with her tongue, encouraging him to fuck her mouth by tugging on his hips with urgent fingers.

She was getting close. He could feel it in the trembling of her thighs, see it in the way her toes were curling. He pulled his tongue from her pussy, holding her steady with one hand while he fingered her ass and nipped at her clit. He kept a steady suction on her clit, tonguing it until she was screeching around him, her orgasm shuddering through her, damn near squeezing his finger off.

He wriggled out from under her, determined to finish what he'd started a month ago. Sinking into her wet heat he rode her hard, more than eager to spill into her warm depths. Bending down he nipped her neck, biting through the skin, tasting her blood on his tongue for the first time.

It was too much for both of them. Lana came with a scream, her pussy walls clamping down so hard on him he was afraid his cock would pop off. His orgasm ripped through him, pouring into her until he had nothing left. He collapsed next to her, pulling her tightly to him. He looked down at his little mate, loving the way she cuddled up against him. He fingered the mark he'd left on her neck, smiling. He whispered the final words to finish the spell and mark her for all time as his. The bite mark turned, twisting, darkening, until the shadow of a black wolf rested on her skin.

She'd accepted him whether she knew it or not. If she hadn't, he could whisper those words for eternity and the shadow would never have shown itself.

His hands stroked down her sweaty back, tangling in her hair again and tugging her mouth to his. His taste mingled with hers, exploding on his tongue. "I've decided something."

She panted on top of him, burying her face against the crook of his neck. "You can think?"

He grinned. "Oh yeah. Want to know my decision?"

"Mmm." She kissed his shoulder, and his cock twitched.

Hell, she *breathed,* and his cock twitched, so that was no surprise. "I could really come to love morning people."

Lana's shoulders stiffened. He waited, continuing to stroke her back, wondering if this was the point where she'd pull away from him, try to put some distance between them. "Could you?"

"I'm certain of it." Hell, he'd already fallen. He just didn't have the courage to tell her yet. She was strong, feisty, funny and the sexiest damn thing he'd ever seen. How could he *not* love her?

Her shoulders relaxed. "See? Mornings aren't all bad, are they?"

"They're becoming my favorite time of the day."

Her head lifted, and she squeaked. "Oh my God!" She leapt out of bed and stumbled, catching herself on the dresser. "Shower. Chris! It's Saturday!"

He sat up, watching her pull a dresser drawer open frantically. "What time do you have to be at Kelly's?"

"Nine a.m."

"Hair and makeup?" His cousin Linda had been a frantic mess just before her wedding when one of her bridesmaids was late for the hair appointment. The maid of honor, his girlfriend at the time, had finally called him to track down the missing girl and drag her to the beauty shop. He still shuddered whenever he thought of his normally cool cousin flipping out with curlers in her hair and half her makeup on, screaming so loud she'd set off a car alarm. She'd looked like...what was the phrase?

Oh yeah. Bridezilla.

He was snapped back to the present by the frantic flapping of his mate. "Yes! Oh Lord. Where's my dress?"

He got out of bed, trying not to laugh at the panic on her face, and went to the closet. "Calm down, sweetheart. Go jump in the shower. I'll have clothes laid out for you and your dress ready to go. You'll just need to grab the right underwear."

"Thanks!" She raced for the bathroom, pausing at the entrance. "Chris?"

"Hmm?" He smiled at her, wondering at the happy expression on her face.

"I could grow to love mornings too." Before he could reply, she shut the door, leaving him standing in the bedroom with what he was certain was the stupidest grin ever to grace a man's face.

She *was* his.

"Stop worrying, everything will be fine." Kerry patted Kelly's hand, their blonde heads close together. "You look beautiful, the bridesmaids look beautiful, and *I* look beautiful. What's left to worry about?"

"That's what you said five minutes ago." Kelly started to bite at her nail, looked at her manicure, and dropped her hand. "Dennis is here, right?"

Kerry sighed. "Yes, Dennis is here. He even looks vaguely humanoid."

Lana rolled her eyes and discreetly stepped on Kerry's foot.

Kerry moved her foot with a strained smile. "Your flowers look great."

The organ music started up behind the closed church doors. Kelly jumped, the panic once more taking over her expression. "Oh God. I'm going to throw up, I just know it."

Lana grabbed Kelly's face. This last-minute hysteria was typical Kelly. "Look at me. He loves you. You love him. You've dreamed about this day, and that man, your whole life. You've had a crush on him since grade school! So get your ass in there and *get married*."

Kelly nodded, the fear fading from her face. "Right." She took a deep breath and blew it out. "I can do this."

The doors swung open, and Lana took her place in line. "Yes, you can." She threw Kelly a kiss and a wink. "Here we go!"

She started down the aisle, smiling at the man standing at the altar. Dennis looked ready to puke himself, his handsome face slightly green, his eyes glued to the doors of the vestry. Beside him his best man was fidgeting, totally ignoring Dennis and the bridal procession.

Lana looked to the left, seeking out Kelly's mom, but before she could find her, she saw Chris. He was seated at the edge of the aisle, close enough to touch her. She walked past with a smile just for him. His expression was full of pride and a wistful longing that damn near brought tears to her eyes. She bit her lip, desperately trying not to let them free. She took her place next to the altar and looked toward the doors as Kerry, the maid of honor, joined her.

The organ music changed to the wedding march, and Kelly stepped into the doorway on the arm of her father. Lana smiled at her friend. The traditional princess-style wedding dress was stunning on her. Lana looked out of the corner of her eye to see Dennis's reaction.

Dennis, old stick in the mud Dennis, was smiling, tears in his eyes. He watched his bride walk down the aisle, so obviously in love the tears Lana had been trying to hold back slipped from her grasp. Visibly trembling, he took Kelly's hand in his, mouthing the words *I love you*. They turned to the priest, Kelly relaxing, her body leaning toward her future husband's. Dennis bent his head toward his future wife protectively. Lana hoped Kerry finally understood what it was that drew Kelly and Dennis, two such opposites, together. The love between the couple was so strong she doubted anything could dim it.

Blinking the tears away, she looked over at Chris, only to find him watching her instead of the wedding. His expression held the same look she'd seen so often on Dennis's face when he looked at Kelly. Protective, possessive, it was full of some indescribable sense of awe, leaving her feeling bubbly and vaguely lightheaded. The butterflies were back in force, but this time they were practically rioting in the pit of her stomach.

Lana reached up and fingered the small golden wolf's head he'd slipped around her neck that morning. The delicate tingle of magic danced under her fingertips. She'd known it for a protection amulet the moment it had touched her skin. She'd been stunned to find out it was his own *personal* amulet, leaving him without some of his protections against Cole.

But she hadn't argued with him. The look in his eyes had been stark. "You wear this. We don't think he has anything personal of yours, but he managed to get to you anyway. If he tries again, I need to know you're protected to the best of my ability, especially while we're out in the open." He'd stroked the wolf's head, his expression fierce. "We'll both keep you safe."

She'd known he'd been talking about his wolf. The intensity he'd shown would have scared her if it had come from anyone other than Chris. She stroked his cheek, smiling when he nuzzled her. "We don't have to go. I could call Kelly, tell her I'm at death's door or something. Maybe it *is* too dangerous, even with all the precautions." She'd been up late the night before, working with Grammy and a curiously helpful Zach to create some protection spells they'd be able to pepper around the wedding party, church and reception. She'd already dropped some of Annabelle's sachets in the limo. The reception area was being seeded with some of the sachets and Lana's protection water by Zach. Chris, Daniel and Gareth had also done their part, creating amulets for everyone to either wear or carry on them. Grammy had also done something for Gareth and Chris, but by the time she'd started it, Lana had been so tired she'd been sent to bed, exhausted from all the spellcasting.

Chris had shaken his head. "No. Besides, the boys will pout if they don't get to use the toys we came up with last night. We've done everything we can think of to make this outing safe. Enjoy it. It might be the last one for a while."

She'd followed him out to his car, waving good-bye to the Beckett brothers already driving away. "You really think Cole will try something?"

The look Chris had shot her as they got into the car said Chris wouldn't put it past the other man.

Frankly, neither would she. Daniel and Zachary had agreed to watch the church from the outside, one seated in his car, the other reading on a bench across from the steps. Gareth was driving around the neighborhood, a crystal dangling from his windshield Grammy had personally spelled. Used for divining over maps, she'd fixed it so the crystal would point to the greatest personal threat toward Chris. Gareth was supposedly following whichever way the crystal swayed, keeping watch for Cole. Grammy was in the back of the church on the groom's side, both she and Christopher ready to act if Cole should try anything within the church itself. They'd agreed to repeat the pattern once they were at the reception. The only time they'd be truly vulnerable would be in transit to the reception. Chris would be driving Lana, the protections wrapped around the car the strongest they could manage, but Kelly and the rest of the wedding party would be vulnerable despite the sachets. She

169

hadn't had time to do a thorough protection spell on the limo itself. They just had to hope that they'd be able to keep up with it and stop anything trying to harm the innocent mundanes riding inside.

It was all they could do in the short amount of time they had, and their best hope of catching Cole out in the open. He'd proven elusive to all of their other methods so far. All enquiries over the last two days had turned up zilch. Until they could either neutralize the threat he represented or the king officially declared someone his heir, their lives would continue to be in danger.

Chris frowned, possibly picking up on her mood, possibly for some obscure wolf reason. She watched him for a moment longer, making sure it wasn't Cole related. Relieved when he shook his head slightly, she tuned back in time to hear Dennis reciting his vows. The bride and groom kissed, to the laughter and applause of their families. She took the arm of her escort and followed the newly married couple out of the church.

Chapter Sixteen

They made it to the reception without incident. It was a lavish affair, everything done in the colors of spring. Pale, multi-hued roses filled the tall vases to near overflowing, greenery draping down the sides to barely kiss the tops of the tables. Votive candles on each setting took the place of candelabra, lending a more casual feel to the otherwise sophisticated décor. White tablecloths, white plates and silver cane back chairs were set up around the head table. Lavender-tinted lighting added another small touch of color. It was feminine without being girly, cultured without being cold, and Chris found himself enchanted. He almost pulled out his PDA to make notes but worried he'd get too caught up in planning his own reception to guard the current one.

Of course, he hoped Lana would pick a different dress than the one the current bride wore. While the poufy skirt and beaded top suited the pale blonde to a T, Lana's dark looks and lush figure called for a simpler dress. He wondered if she'd let him go shopping with her to pick it out.

Of course, that would depend on whether or not she agreed to get married. He couldn't plan a wedding with a reluctant bride, no matter how much he might wish to do so. He just hoped he'd be able to talk her into it. Marrying the woman he loved, putting the symbol on her finger that even a human could see and know she was taken, was a dream he found himself indulging now in ways he'd never thought possible.

He wanted every possible bond with her. He wanted her last name changed to his. He desperately wanted the joint checking account, the mortgage, the two-car garage. The children, the laughter, the fights, he wanted everything that would declare to the world she was his mate, his wife, his family.

He watched her sway to the music, her escort keeping a respectful distance between their bodies. The lavender, high waist dress brought out the dark depths of her eyes, the material flowing around her legs. He caught a glimpse of her toes through her shoes, the nails painted a bright red.

"If you drool any more you'll be panting."

Chris tore his eyes away from Lana long enough to glare at Gareth. "What are you doing in here?"

"Eating. Nice spread. Remind me to kiss the bride later." Gareth popped one of the canapés into his mouth. "Damn crystal hung straight down. It didn't even move when I took corners. If he's here then he's blocking even such a simple divination."

"Either that or he's not a threat to *me* right now."

Gareth paused, another canapé halfway to his lips. "Well. Fuck."

"Here." He took a second crystal, this one made of chocolate quartz, and handed it to his brother. He'd asked Grammy to make it after Lana had gone to bed, tired from her own spellcasting. "Do another check. This one's tuned to Lana."

"On it." Gareth left, but not before swiping one more canapé off of Chris's plate.

He turned his attention toward Lana. She was laughing up

at her escort, her head thrown back, her amazing breasts threatening to spill out of the top of her dress.

Chris was in front of the other man before he'd even realized he'd moved. "Mind if I cut in?"

The man pulled away, a look of amusement on his face, his hands in the air. "She's all yours. Later, Lana."

Chris turned and pulled Lana into his arms, his eyes roaming to where he knew his shadow mark now rested on her neck. The knowledge that she'd finally acknowledged their mating raced through him, filling him with happiness beyond any he'd ever known.

He pulled Lana into his arms, much tighter than the other man had held her, and began dancing. "Have I told you how beautiful you look tonight?"

"Not yet." She cupped her ear and tilted her head to the side, her expression waiting.

"You look beautiful tonight."

Her arm went around her neck. "Thank you. You don't look half bad yourself."

"I wore the Armani just for you."

Her stunned expression quickly turned to horrified laughter. "Oh no you didn't."

"What, you didn't recognize it?"

"Chris!"

"I smell your skin every time I move." She gulped, her cheeks heating. He placed a soft kiss on her neck, loving the way her head moved just enough to accommodate him. "I might never have it cleaned again."

"You are so bad." She leaned back, her smile soft and sultry and just a tad indulgent.

Her expression made his heart soar. He loved her so much

173

he could barely breathe. "But you like me that way."

"Mmm. True." She didn't protest when his hand slid down to rest at the curve of her ass. "What am I going to do with you?"

Love me. Please love me. "What would you like to do with me?"

"Could I do anything I wanted?"

He blinked. "Anything is such a *broad* term."

She giggled. "Could I...convince you to get a tattoo?"

One eyebrow rose. "A tattoo."

Her head tilted. "Yup. A tattoo."

"How many champagnes have you had?"

"Not *that* many. C'mon. Could I?"

"Like tattoos, do you?"

"Maybe," she drawled, drawing her finger up and down his shoulder.

He narrowed his eyes thoughtfully. If the thought of a tattoo brought such a dark flush to her cheeks, he'd definitely have to get inked. "I suppose I could accommodate you. What would you like to see?"

"Wow. You gave in easily for a man with no ink on him."

He waited for the answer to his question.

"Fine. A witch would be nice. Maybe Wendy from Caspar?"

No fucking way. "A witch, yes. Wendy, no." No way was he walking around with a cartoon witch on his anything. "If I get a witch tattooed on me, you bet your sweet ass it will be the real deal." He already had an idea, something that would please them both and mark him unmistakably as hers.

She studied him thoughtfully. "Why do I get the feeling you might have something in mind already?"

"Because you're a very smart woman who is beginning to know me too well?"

"Good answer." Her expression turned serious. "How's the search for Cole going?"

"Nothing so far. Gareth's trying a different tack. I don't know whether to hope we actually find the bastard or go home empty-handed."

She patted his hand, the one currently holding on to her butt. "Not completely empty-handed."

He threw his head back and laughed, squeezing her ass cheek a little tighter. "Nope, not empty-handed at all."

"So, who's studlicious?" Kerry was grinning at her, champagne in one hand and her hair clip in the other. Her hair had tumbled down during a particularly enthusiastic dance with one of Kerry's young cousins, not that Kerry seemed to mind. Now the carefully crafted curls tumbled wildly about her face. She looked like a demented debutante.

"Studlicious, as you put it, is Chris Beckett." Lana's eyes were drawn to Chris. He was standing in the corner of the room, talking to one of the groomsmen, his gaze constantly tracking around the room. When he found her, he smiled, hefting his glass to her before turning to his companion.

"New boyfriend?" Lana turned to find Kerry checking Chris out. "Mommy approves. What does he do for a living?"

"He's a graphics artist for Black Wolf."

"Cool. The Armani says he makes good money. Is he packing?"

"Kerry!"

Kerry turned to her. "What?" She glanced back at Chris, her expression wicked. "I'd hate to think a sundae that yummy didn't have a cherry on top."

"Let me put it to you this way, baby bear. He's juuust right."

"Really?" Kerry's head tilted to the side. "Does he have any brothers?"

She sipped from her champagne before answering. "Three."

Kerry batted her lashes. "Invite me to the next family barbeque? Please?"

"Kerry—"

"I'll pay for your next pedicure."

"Done." She wondered how the Beckett brothers would react to her brash, outspoken friend. It would be fun finding out. Kerry was her best friend, so they'd better get used to her.

An arm snaked around her waist. "Hey, sweetheart. Having a good time?"

Chris's deep voice washed over her. She shivered, her body heating up at the feel of his warm body curling around hers. "Yup. You?"

A kiss landed on her neck. "It's a lot better now."

"He's good." Kerry held out her hand with a laugh. "Kerry Andrews."

"Christopher Beckett. Nice to meet you."

"Nice to meet you too." She turned her head. "They're getting ready to throw the bouquet!" She grabbed Lana's arm. "C'mon!"

Lana allowed herself to be dragged along behind Kerry, laughing at Kerry's enthusiasm. They took their place in line with the other single women, eagerly waiting for Kelly to toss her bouquet. She ignored the glare Chris was sending her way, stretching her arms up and screeching with the other girls when the flowers flew overhead.

They landed in Lana's arms with a thump. She clutched them to her chest, startled; she'd intended to direct them Kerry's way. *Oops.*

"Darn it." Kerry pouted briefly before grinning. "Looks like Chris might be the one after all, you lucky, lucky girl." Kerry rubbed her hands together and backed away from the dance floor. "Let's see who gets the garter."

Christopher stood in line with the other single men, determined that not one of them would claim the prize and touch Lana's sweet flesh. He had every intention of using maiming tactics if he had to.

From the smirk on Annabelle's face he had a pretty good idea how Lana had gotten the bouquet so easily. If anyone could manipulate thrown flowers without causing a ripple in the magical stream, it would be Annabelle.

He figured she planned on making sure he got the garter. He was all for helping her along, even if he had to cheat.

The garter was tossed, and Christopher jumped, snagging it in midair. From the shocked look on everyone's faces he might have been a smidge *too* enthusiastic, but what the hell.

He led Lana over to the seat and slid her shoe off, stroking her instep with his finger. She wiggled and jerked, glaring at him, daring him to do it again.

Mm. Ticklish spot. I'll have to remember that for later.

Ignoring the raucous calls of the crowd and the sexy teasing of the DJ, he placed her foot on his knee. Sliding the garter slowly up her leg, savoring the soft feel of her skin, he watched her, his gaze tangling with hers, keeping her focused only on him and what his hands were doing. Her face flushed darker and darker the farther up her leg he got. He slid it up to mid-thigh and stopped. Her breathing hitched, and she gulped.

His fingers flexed on her soft skin, reminding her of what his touch could do to her.

His hands drifted down, lifting her foot to his lips. He kissed her ankle and slid her shoe back on, the dazed expression on her face a fitting payment for the blue balls he was sure he would have until he could get her home and into his bed. He stood and helped her from the chair, the clapping and laughter of the guests surrounding them.

Lana hid her face against his chest. "You are so bad."

He grinned wickedly and dipped her. "And you like me that way." He stole a kiss from her, beyond grateful when she immediately kissed him back.

When he managed to pull away from her lips, the expression on her face had his heart stuttering in his chest. Full of warmth and want and laughter, it made him want to whisk her away from everyone and everything and explore whatever it was lighting her up from within.

Instead he stood, twirling her and taking a bow to her friends and family. She got it immediately, curtseying to the crowd before dragging him off the dance floor. She led him past Kerry, laughing when the blonde fanned herself. "This is a hell of a first date, Chris."

He stumbled. It wasn't how he'd envisioned their first date going, but somehow...somehow, it was perfect. He squeezed Lana's hand. She looked at him, so full of happiness she glowed with it.

Absolutely perfect.

"Christopher!"

He turned to find Zachary running toward him, his expression panicked.

"Zach?"

"Gareth's hurt bad."

He didn't even stop to think. He ran.

"Who's Gareth?" He was startled to hear Kerry's voice at his elbow.

They shoved open the door to the reception hall and ran into the parking lot. "My brother."

"Crap." The blonde put on an extra burst of speed, impressive in the heels she was wearing. She actually reached the bloodied man on the street before he did, going to her knees and assessing the damage in a professional manner that screamed experience. "Call nine-one-one," she ordered, pushing Daniel out of her way without a second glance. Daniel allowed himself to be pushed, but from the look on his face he was none too happy about it.

Christopher had never felt so helpless in all his life. "What can I do to help?"

Kerry checked Gareth over, her face turning grim. "Think happy thoughts."

Christopher pulled out his phone and dialed.

Chapter Seventeen

"He'll be all right, Chris." Lana hugged Chris, pulling him down onto the hard plastic seat. He'd been pacing since Gareth went into surgery.

"If he'd been two inches shorter his throat would be slit." Her wolf was growling. Rage poured off of him in palpable waves. "I'm going to kill him."

She didn't even have to wonder whose death he was contemplating. "Cole can't get away with this. The karma alone is going to be a bitch."

"Thank the Goddess your friend Kerry was there." He shuddered. "I don't know what we would have done without her."

She stroked his hair, sighing when he relaxed into her. "Called an ambulance and held a cloth to the wound, same as she did."

"He's going to make it."

"Yes, he is. Don't doubt it for a second." Because if Gareth didn't make it, she had no idea what Chris would do.

"How the fuck did this happen?" Zach growled. His blue eyes were dark with worry. The youngest Beckett was pacing the worn linoleum, tension riding his lean frame.

Lana stared blearily at Zach. She was so damn tired. "I'm

not exactly sure."

"There's no fucking way Gareth would drive with an open switchblade on the dashboard and you know it." Zach was practically vibrating. Lana wondered if she had the strength to deal with all of the Beckett males.

"We already know Gareth isn't stupid. We also know stomping on the brakes plain old *can't* drive a knife into a man so hard it penetrates his collar bone and sticks there." Daniel cracked his knuckles, his eyes never leaving the swinging doors the doctors would come through after surgery. "The knife was shoved into him by someone or something."

Kerry snorted. "The man was locked in his car, no broken windows, no nothing. If he got stabbed it was because he stabbed himself."

"Or the attacker was already in the car with him." Daniel cracked another knuckle.

"The angle of the knife tells me it came dead on from the top of the steering wheel. I'm not sure an assailant could even angle his arm the right way to get make that kind of a wound, not without rubber arms and gorilla strength."

Daniel finally turned his glare onto something other than the doors. "You stay out of this. You have no idea what you're dealing with."

Kerry leaned toward Daniel. "Magic. Woo-woo stuff. Right?" She wiggled her fingers in his face, ignoring his shocked look. "Lana's my *best* friend. Whatever is going on here involves her, therefore it involves me. And the angle of the knife wound indicates that it came out of the steering wheel of the car. What if Lana had been driving? She'd be *dead.* So get over yourself, get over the fact that I'm a *mundane,* and let's all assume that Kerry has a brain in her pretty blonde head. 'Kay?" She patted Daniel on the head like a dog, nearly earning herself a bite from the normally unflappable Daniel.

Lana was shocked. She'd never told any of the Andrews what she was. How had Kerry known? "Kerry?"

Kerry turned to Lana with a sigh. "You really think you could hide that from me? Seriously? I had a nice long talk with Grammy when we were sixteen, and she told me everything." Kerry shook her head, an echo of an old hurt deep in her eyes. "I understand why you didn't tell me, but I wish you'd trusted me."

Lana blinked away tears. "I couldn't, not without permission. But I wish I had too."

Kerry nodded. "So. A spell, right? Who was the target?"

"We're not sure." Chris cuddled Lana closer, kissing the tears from her cheeks. "We do know who cast it."

"Cole." Lana shuddered. "I'm really beginning to hate that man."

"You and me both, sweetheart."

Kerry plopped down on the seat, the satin of her dress crackling against the plastic cushion. "So what now?"

"Now you keep your pretty ass out of it." Daniel was still glaring at Kerry. He actually growled at her when Kerry flipped him off. "I mean it. You have even less defenses against Cole than Lana does. Do you understand me?"

"Actually, there may be something I can do about it." Grammy stepped over to Kerry. "Do you still have the charm Lana gave you for your eighteenth birthday?"

Kerry nodded. "In my jewelry case back home. Why?"

Grammy smiled wearily. "It was a gift of love from a dear friend. If I can borrow it for a day or two, I can enchant it to protect you from those who would wish you harm. Would that be all right?"

"Yes. Thank you, Grammy." Kerry's smile was tinged with relief. "I want to help Lana, even if it means helping Mr. Grumpypants."

Daniel took one step toward Kerry. What he intended to do when he reached her was a mystery, because the surgeon came out of the swinging doors and captured his complete attention. "Christopher Beckett?"

"Here." Chris stood, holding on to Lana with everything in him.

"Your brother is going to be just fine. Frankly, if the knife had hit him just slightly to the left he'd be dead right now, so he's a very lucky young man. We're keeping him overnight for observation, and he'll have to undergo some physical therapy to get full use of his arm back, but I think he'll make a full recovery."

"Thank the Lady." Lana turned Chris and hugged him, his body sagging against her in relief.

"Now that we know Gareth will be all right, why don't you come with me, Kerry? We'll take care of the protection charm, and you'll be able to change your clothes." Grammy gave each of the Beckett brothers a hug before tugging Kerry out of the hospital waiting room.

"When will your parents get here?" Lana forced Chris to sit. He still looked a little gray to her.

"They were in Chicago at a seminar. They're still trying to get a flight." He rubbed his face wearily. "It could have been you in the car, Lana."

She shook her head. "I don't think we were the targets. Not this time. I think it was a message."

He looked at her through his fingers. "Sort of 'I can get you anywhere, anytime'?"

"Yeah." She rubbed Chris's back, hoping to soothe him.

He clenched his jaw, his pupils widening until his eyes were small golden rings around a sea of black. "Message received."

Lana went down to breakfast Sunday morning to find three of the four Beckett brothers seated at Christopher's table. She wondered if Gareth's pain medication had made him sleep in, or if he'd already been down to eat and gone back to bed. She was pretty certain it was the former.

Getting the oldest Beckett brother to move in temporarily had been a battle all on its own. He'd wanted to return to his home in Pittsburgh, feeling he would only be in the way now that he was groggy on pain meds. She and Chris had talked him into staying with them. Chris had argued he'd feel safer knowing Gareth was there to protect Lana if anything happened to him, swaying the tide in their favor. He'd totally worked Gareth's overdeveloped protective streak to their advantage, and while Gareth obviously knew it he'd stopped objecting.

So far, nothing had happened, thank the Lord and Lady. She didn't know if Cole was laying low after the attack at the wedding, or preparing for one hell of a spell. Either way having the Beckett brothers so close made guarding everyone that much easier.

She turned her eyes to Chris. Her wolf looked grumpy this morning, swatting Zach's hand away from the last piece of toast with a low growl. "Save some for my mate, you heathen."

"Speaking of which, good morning, Lana." Daniel stood, pulling out her chair for her.

Chris took one look at her still wearing his shirt and frowned. "Why aren't you dressed?"

"Thank you." She took the seat gingerly, waiting until Daniel sat down. "It's Pajama Sunday."

Chris blinked, a slow frown forming on his face. "Pajama Sunday."

"Yup." She snagged the last piece of toast and nibbled on it delicately. "I get to sit around in my jammies, watch television, and generally make a pig of myself."

Chris chuckled. "I like it already."

Zach ducked his head under the table. "Are you wearing underwear?"

"Zachary!" Chris yanked his brother up by the hair.

"Pig!" Lana threw her napkin at him.

"I am not a pig. I'm a growing boy. Can't you tell?" Zachary flexed his muscles, throwing her a happy puppy look.

His happy puppy look changed to a grumble when Daniel snagged Zachary's last piece of bacon. "We hope some day he'll even grow a brain."

Zach picked up the napkin she'd thrown at him and threw it at Daniel. "What is with you and stealing my food?"

Zachary slapped his hands over his plate. Daniel smirked. "I'm a growing boy."

Lana bit her lip to keep from laughing. Chris's head was in his hands, but she could see his shoulders shaking. Whether they were shaking from laughter or sobs she couldn't tell.

"Could you two idiots go call Mom and Dad and let them know what's going on? They're at the Holiday Inn, room two-fifteen." Chris stood, taking the dirty plates from the table into the kitchen.

Zachary and Daniel stared at Chris. "Me? Call *Mom*?" Zach pointed to Chris. "She's your mate, you should call."

Chris glared at Zach from the kitchen sink. "I'm *not* calling

185

Mom and telling her Cole threatened my mate. Besides, I told her one of you would call with an update on Gareth."

Daniel began backing slowly toward the patio door. "Don't even think of asking me to do it."

Zach stood. "Run?"

Daniel nodded. "Run."

They ran, right out the door and straight onto the patio, shedding clothes as they went. Lana tried to peek around Chris to see the brothers disrobing, but he kept blocking her view.

"Party pooper." She folded her arms over her chest and pouted for all she was worth. She laughed when he growled at her.

She stopped laughing when he picked her up and tossed her over his shoulder. She felt something sharp digging into her side. *Claws?* She twisted, trying to see his hand, but the smart smack he gave her butt stopped her. "You want to see a naked Beckett?"

She gulped and stilled. There was a deep, growling quality to his usually smooth voice that warned her to be very careful. She wasn't afraid he would hurt her, but it was better not to tug on the wolf's tail.

His hand caressed her bare ass. "Fucking naked under my shirt." And he took off, carting her up the stairs so quickly the walls blurred. When they got to his bedroom, he slammed the door shut hard enough to rattle the walls. "No underwear. Trying to see my brothers' bare asses. Parading around in front of them in nothing but my shirt. Are you trying to drive me insane?" Claws gently scraped her naked ass, his palm rough against her skin.

"Uh, wait?" She blinked. *Why did it come out as a question?*

He placed her on her feet, his expression full of heated lust.

His hands drifted up her thighs, the cool rasp of his claws somehow heightening her arousal. She backed away, her gaze never leaving his heated expression.

And she was aroused. There was no denying it. Something about the feral way he was stalking her across the bedroom heated her blood.

Her back hit the wall. She'd run out of room.

His hands came to rest on either side of her head. "You like to tease, sweetheart?"

She licked her lips, her heart hammering in her chest. "Sometimes." She wasn't exactly fighting what he was about to do to her. In fact, she was looking forward to it. They could both use the relief a bout of hot, sweaty sex could give them. Still, she was in the mood to play a little. She resisted the urge to reach out and trace the muscles of his chest. She knew now exactly how hard and hot those muscles were, how they would twitch under the stroke of her fingers.

He reached out and cupped her breast through his shirt. "I like to tease too." His thumb stroked over her nipple, bringing it to aching life. His lips curled in a sensuous smile. "But do you know what I like most of all?"

She shook her head, more than half her attention on his hand.

He tweaked her nipple between his thumb and finger. "I like to make my women scream."

Her eyes narrowed as she snarled at him. *Women?*

He laughed, obviously delighted with her response. "Woman." He reached down and lightly stroked her clit. "I bet I could make you too."

Everything in her bristled. "Oh no. I bet I could make *you*."

"You're on."

She blinked. Had she just agreed to...?

Oh. *Oh.*

His finger had slipped between her slippery folds, stroking her clit in light, teasing touches. Her hips snapped forward all on their own, trying to bring him closer, to rub harder on that maddening digit.

She opened her mouth, to say what, she wasn't sure. It wasn't like he gave her a chance to say anything. His tongue was in her mouth so fast he was lucky she didn't bite him by accident. But then he started doing things with his tongue, his lips, that *finger,* driving every thought out of her head but one.

Time to play.

Chapter Eighteen

She reached down and cupped him through his jeans, his soft groan music to her ears. She unzipped him, pulling his cock out into her hand. She stroked up and down the shaft, jacking him while he slipped his finger inside her, slowly fucking her.

He pulled away from her mouth with a moan, latching onto her breast through the shirt, suckling at her nipple, until she was gasping, riding his hand, almost ready to beg.

He pulled out of her, smirking at her whimper. He sucked her juices from his finger, growling when she pulled her hand from his cock and lapped *his* juices from *her* fingers. He ripped the shirt open, scattering buttons and exposing her naked breasts, the nipples beaded and hard.

Before he could do much more than look, she was on her knees, sucking him into her mouth. His taste was divine, salty and sweet. She lapped him up, savoring him.

"Holy fuck." He wrapped a hand around the back of her head, holding her steady while he pumped between her lips. The other was on the wall, his back hunched, his head bowed. He watched himself slide in and out of her lips with a rapt expression. She held still, allowing him to control the pace of the blowjob, stroking his shaft with her tongue, determined to get him to scream first.

She peeked up at him and saw his jaw clench. He was watching her face, his gaze drifting between her eyes and mouth. When she closed her eyes and hummed, he pulled out with a gasp.

"Oh, no you don't." He sounded breathless. He pulled her up by the arms and began walking her backward toward the bed. "You're very good."

She smirked. "Thank you."

His gaze darkened. "I'm the only one whose cock you'll be sucking from now on."

She decided not to say anything. He had that possessive look on his face again, the one she now knew was directed only at her. He hadn't even glanced at another woman at the reception, and Kerry's beauty had garnered no response.

He picked her up and laid her on the bed, his shirt spread under her. Neither one of them had bothered taking the ruined shirt off of her. Her legs dangled over the side, her feet hanging above the carpet, her legs nudged apart by his thighs. When he went down on his knees, her pussy clenched in anticipation. She expected him to go right for her clit. Most of her previous lovers had. But not Chris. Instead, he began slowly lapping at her, from her hole to her clit, steady, rhythmically. Maddeningly. Her body began to ride his tongue, the rasp of his whiskers against her inner thighs just intensifying the sensation. Over and over and over, he licked his way up and down, up and down until she was completely drenched and desperate to come. She reached up and began tweaking at her breasts, pulling on her nipples, thrusting against his face. His hands held her thighs apart, his fingers digging into her flesh, his low, hungry growls throwing her over the edge.

She bit her lip to keep from screaming. The orgasm washed over her, so intense she saw spots dancing in front of her eyes.

It felt like forever before the spasms ended, but when they did he was still there, kneeling between her thighs, lapping at her, drinking in her juices, lightly trying to drive her back up again.

She whimpered and her body began to stir once more under his expert touch. When he took her hands and put them on her breasts, she eagerly began playing with them again. This time, when he pushed her over the edge, she clutched his head, holding him right where she wanted him, riding his mouth. She moaned out her pleasure, her back bowing, and her fist pounding the mattress.

Sated, tired, she merely groaned when he lifted her up and placed her on her stomach. Her hips were lifted into the air and a pillow placed beneath them. She heard the sounds of his clothes hitting the floor. His weight hit the bed, almost rolling her over. She steadied herself, giggling, turning tired eyes to see him in all his naked glory. He was magnificent. All corded muscle and smooth, tanned skin, with a washboard stomach and a cock to die for. Thick and red, it jutted out from the nest of black curls, the tip glistening with pre-come.

He draped himself over her, teasing her with his cock. "Ready to scream?"

She waved one hand languidly, already knowing he wouldn't get much more out of her. Her body was still humming lightly from the last orgasm. "I think I'm done. But you go ahead." *You've earned it.*

He reached between their bodies, pinching her clit. She gasped, the sensation rocketing through her. "You think you're done, sweetheart? Because I don't." He smiled against her neck, breathing into her ear, "You *will* come, and you will come *hard.*"

She shivered. Her nipples, the little traitors, perked right up, ready and willing for round three. Her pussy quivered in response to his deep growl. When his teeth grazed the back of her neck she quivered.

His smile deepened against her skin as his cock slipped inside her. He nibbled at her neck, sucking up a mark she knew would last for days. He rode her slow and easy, his body hunched over hers, watching her as he took her. He continued to pluck at her clit until her body was bucking into him, eager for more. The fabric of the comforter scraped against her nipples, heightening her arousal.

And then she looked up, turning her head to get a better look at him, and froze. The way he'd positioned them, she could see everything in the old-fashioned standing mirror next to the bed. Him, sliding in and out of her, his cock red and straining. Her, back bowed, inviting his teeth, his fingers, his cock, her face full of lust, her lips red and swollen from kisses.

And his eyes, those golden eyes, glued to hers through the fall of his bangs in the mirror. He fucked her like there was no place else on earth he needed to be ever again.

She panted, bucking into him harder, tightening the muscles of her pussy until he flinched. His expression turned desperate, and his body lost the slow, lazy rhythm he'd set up until he was fucking her so hard she thought he might leave bruises. He pounded into her, snarling over her, releasing her clit to grab hold of both of her hips.

She began to stroke herself, the urge to come intensifying with each move of his cock inside her. She could feel it building, her body quivering, straining toward fulfillment.

"Come." He nuzzled against the back of her neck, the scrape of his teeth turning into the burn of a bite. She shrieked, coming around him in the most colossal orgasm she'd ever experienced in her life. It shot through her, robbing her of breath, of thought, more brutally satisfying than anything she'd experienced in her entire fucking life.

His own roar of completion was partially muffled against her neck, his arms clenched around her waist to hold her in place while he emptied himself inside her.

She collapsed onto the bed, completely rung out. He flopped down beside her, both of them covered in sweat.

"So who won?"

He laughed silently, rolling her over until her body was cradled against him. She drifted off to sleep before hearing his answer.

The first thing he noticed was the ringing of the phone. The second was the warm, damp female body spooned in his arms. He smiled sleepily, wondering when they'd rearranged themselves. He kind of liked the new position, the feel of her delectable ass snuggled up against his growing erection.

"You gonna answer that?"

He pulled her closer to him and mumbled into her hair, "No." He licked his mark, delighted when she shivered. "M'busy."

Someone pounded on his bedroom door. "Christopher! Answer the God damn phone!"

Christopher groaned. "Go the fuck away!"

"Just check the caller ID!"

Christopher rolled over and took a look at the phone. The number had him sitting up, his hard-on deflating. He picked up the phone. "Cole."

"Christopher."

That hated voice rolled over him. He gritted his teeth, trying to hold his wolf's instinctual desire to growl at the man who had not only threatened his mate but his pack. "What do you want?"

Dana Marie Bell

"I understand your brother had an accident. Pity, but the Neanderthal doesn't really need his head, does he?"

"He's fine, actually. Thank you for calling." Christopher waved Lana away but she didn't take the hint, curling up against him and trying to hear Cole's end of the conversation.

"Really? How marvelous. Congratulations on your mating, by the way."

He growled, his wolf dangerously close to the surface. "You leave my woman out of this."

Cole chuckled. "A witch, Christopher? Truly? How...droll."

Lana's hands wrapped around his neck, her ear pressing against the receiver in an attempt to hear the conversation. "My little witch took care of your storm, didn't she?"

She kissed the side of his neck and pressed her ear back to the receiver.

"Alannah took out the storm?" Cole's laugh was strained, a sound filled with absolutely no humor. "Well, it seems she has some power. Perhaps I should challenge her, see what she's made of, especially since she assaulted me first."

"What?" Christopher felt his wolf trying to slip its leash, eager to protect their mate from Cole's threat.

"You heard me. She assaulted me first. The branch that fell on my head and knocked me out? I know it was her, not you. That grants me the right to challenge."

Christopher snarled. "You stay away from her or I will rip your prick off and shove it up your ass."

"Are you threatening me?"

"No. I think you secretly like having things shoved up your ass. I'm just being neighborly."

Lana buried her face in his shoulder, stifling a giggle.

"I know she's there, Christopher. Put her on the phone so I

194

can formally challenge her."

Christopher saw red. "I will kill you first."

"Ah, a definite threat." Christopher could practically hear the smile in Cole's voice, but couldn't bring himself to care. "I challenge you to a duel, Christopher Beckett."

"Accepted." He ignored the tightening of Lana's arms, concentrating solely on Cole.

"And when your corpse lies on the field, I'll take your woman and fuck her until she bleeds."

The phone shattered in Christopher's hands.

"Whoa." Lana stared at the wreck of the phone. "What did he say to piss you off?"

He turned to face her, the red haze of anger still coating everything. "I have a duel to prepare for."

"What?"

He climbed out of bed, pulling her along behind him. "We need a shower, then we need to go consult with my brothers." There was no way in hell he was leaving her alone, either here at the house or at the duel. His brothers would have to guard her while he fought. She followed him docilely into the bathroom. He wished he could enjoy the view, but damn it if Cole's phone call hadn't killed his libido.

"What the fuck is that?"

He turned to find her staring in the mirror, her eyes tracing the black wolf on her neck. "My mark."

She glared at him in the mirror. "Your mark."

He smiled smugly. "You are my mate. All of the Beckett mates wear the mark."

"I never agreed to be your mate!"

He was stunned. Hurt. "Yes, you did."

"When?" Her hands went on her hips, her foot tapping.

"'Knot of eight protect my mate.'"

The foot stopped. Her mouth fell open. Her hands fell to her sides. A blush crept up her chest to her face. "Oh."

"Yes, oh. I think, consider your spell, it's safe to say I assumed I had your consent." She *couldn't* reject him now. Could she?

"It would have been nice to be asked," she muttered.

He sniffed, ignoring her. He tested the temperature of the water with his wrist, wanting the water just right. He wasn't done being pissed yet, but he wanted to relax with his mate before he damn well exploded from stress.

"I didn't realize."

"Realize what?"

She sighed and wrapped her arms around his waist. "When I did the knot spell I did it on the fly."

His hands stalled. He felt dizzy. He could not have just heard what he'd heard. "What?"

"I mean, I knew what I needed, I just didn't know the words, you know? Not the exact ones, anyway."

Her hands were stroking his chest, but he didn't feel it. All he could feel was the new gray hair sprouting on his head. His heart pounded in fear. His little witch had stopped Cole with a *made up spell?* Did she have any *idea* what could have happened to her? He stood to his full height, turning to face her. She flinched, and he knew his wolf was closer to the surface than he'd thought.

"What? It worked, didn't it?"

No fear. Not one single ounce of fear in her. Defiance, a hint of remorse, but that was it.

Chris growled, and it wasn't human. His wolf had taken

over, and it was *pissed.* Lana gasped, backing away from him, from his anger. He shifted, needing to run, needing to get away before he said something or did something he'd regret. He went to the window, pressing a specially made latch with his paw. The window swung open and he leapt out into the mid-afternoon sun.

"Chris, wait! Please!"

He ignored her, running into the forest, intent on taking out his rage on some poor, defenseless rabbits rather than her soft, sweet skin.

Chapter Nineteen

"You did *what?*" Daniel, obviously astonished, ran his fingers through his hair.

"Damn, no wonder he's pissed." Gareth shook his head at her, his expression somewhere between reluctant admiration and anger. He looked the worse for wear, his arm in a sling to protect his collar bone, the stitches near the knife wound black against his golden skin. He lounged on the sofa, his feet up, looking pale and pissed.

"Pass the peanuts, dickhead. Stop hogging them." Zachary pulled the bowl toward him, smiling happily.

"She could have been killed, idiot." Daniel snatched the bowl away, ignoring his brother's whine. "She's lucky Christopher didn't spank her ass and tie her to the bed."

"Or worse." Gareth looked at his brothers. "Mom."

They shuddered.

Lana slouched deeper into the chair. Two of the brothers definitely were taking Christopher's side, and she just couldn't understand why. "What did I do that was so bad, anyway?"

They looked at her with blank astonishment. Gareth broke the silence. "You never, *ever* use an untested spell! It's the first thing drummed into our heads when we're still in diapers!"

"You had no idea what components he'd used to cast the

original spell, so your counter-spell could have interacted poorly and blown up in your face, or worse, made *his* spell stronger." Daniel began pacing, ticking points off on his fingers. "You didn't scry to see what protections he'd put up. Again, this could have lead to your spell blowing up in your face. Placement of the counter-spell needs to be laid out precisely." Daniel threw his hands up in the air. "Frankly, I'm surprised you're still alive."

"I'm not." Zach handed her a peanut.

Lana took it. "Thank you."

Daniel snorted. "Of course you aren't. You'd have done the same harebrained thing, and we'd be explaining to Mom how you wound up smeared all over Christopher's back yard. Even then I'm not sure you can pull it off. Sorry, but of the four of us you're the weakest, bro."

Zachary looked ticked for a moment before picking up the peanut bowl, his usual sunny smile once more in place. "You're just mad because a girl kicked Cole's ass."

Lana watched them arguing, but her attention remained on Zachary. Something about the youngest Beckett had her instincts hopping to attention. The strange reference in The Registry popped into her mind.

Was it possible the youngest Beckett wasn't a wizard after all?

When the other brothers weren't looking, Zach flicked his finger. A peanut, physically untouched, went flying out of the bowl and struck Daniel in the back of the head.

Daniel turned and glared at his brother. "Did you just throw a peanut at me, you juvenile twat?"

Gareth sighed. "Like calling him a twat is more adult?"

"I'm not the one starting a food fight!" And they were off

again, squabbling like...well, family.

With a soft smile Lana pointed her finger at the peanut bowl. Three peanuts jumped into the air and pelted the brothers. When they turned to her, she smiled. "Shut the fuck up." She stood. "We have more important things to worry about, like how Christopher is going to beat Cole." *And how to break it to Zach that he's a witch, not a wizard.* She would double-check in The Registry, make sure what she'd seen and what she'd read matched, but her instincts were usually dead on.

If Zach was a wizard, she'd eat her favorite pair of lace panties.

"I think you should stay out of it. You've done enough." Daniel's voice was cold.

"Leave her alone." Zach, bless his heart, got in between his brothers and her. "She did something none of the rest of us could do. She broke Cole's spell before someone got hurt. She's also Christopher's mate, so she's a Beckett, whether your dumb ass likes it or not."

She tapped Zach on the shoulder. "Actually, I think *you* would have been just fine." She hitched a thumb at Gareth and Daniel. "They, on the other hand, would have been paste."

Daniel made a rude noise. "Sorry, but Zach is barely strong enough to qualify as a wizard."

"Prick!" Zach started to lunge, but Lana's hand on his shoulder stopped him.

"Which just means Zach is one of the most powerful *witches* I've ever met."

The brothers, shocked, froze.

"Excuse me?" Zach turned to face her. *"Witch?"*

She nodded, seeing the longing, the need, inside him. She bet he'd found trying to be a wizard more than a little frustrating. The fact he'd accomplished anything at all told her just how powerful he must be, but she didn't want him to know too much too soon. Not until Grammy had a look at him. "You'll need to be assessed, but I'm betting you'll grade fairly high on the scale." *Actually, you might* break *the scale.*

Zach gulped, his eyes wide.

Daniel laughed.

She wanted to smack Daniel when Zach's eyes filled with hurt.

But when they filled with anger...when he turned to his brother...

She stepped between Daniel and Zach and placed her hand on Zach's chest. "No!" She pulled his face down to hers. "Anger is what cursed the Becketts. *Never* cast in anger." She waited until she saw he'd acknowledged that, breathing deep, reigning in the rage.

"I wouldn't have."

She might have believed him if he hadn't been talking through clenched teeth. "Take hold of your anger. Dilute it. Channel it. Allow it to fuel you, but never allow it to *use* you." She huffed. "A witch gets a stronger boost the more they feel. Love, anger, hate, determination, all of it fuels your gift, but if you allow it to *rule* your gift, you will find yourself on the wrong end of the karma stick. Got it?"

"Karma stick?" Zach's lips twitched, the tension in his shoulders easing.

"The witch who cursed you? She's a giant bunny."

Zach blinked, swallowing hard. "Bunny?"

"Her great great-great-blah-blah grandchildren are *serious* vegetarians."

Zach collapsed into a chair, laughing his ass off.

"You really think he's a witch?" Gareth was frowning at them, but he looked intrigued.

She nodded. "Yes."

"How do you know?" Daniel still sounded hostile, but some of the wind had gone out of his sails.

She grinned slowly. "Let's just say it takes one to know one." She flicked her finger, and every peanut in the bowl landed on Daniel.

She slid her arm through Zach's and hauled him to his feet, ignoring both Daniel's sputtering and Gareth's laughter. "Come along, Zach. You and I have someone to talk to." She led the still chuckling Zach out of the room and went looking for Annabelle. Grammy was going to love this. A Beckett witch?

Zach's parents were going to shit a cow.

Christopher returned from his run to find Gareth and Daniel sitting quietly in his office, waiting for him. The Registry lay open between them, the picture of Zach smiling up at them. "What's wrong?"

Daniel glared at him. "When were you going to tell us Zach is a witch?"

Christopher sighed. He so did not need this shit right now. "I'm not sure. Did you read the entry?"

Gareth looked like he'd bitten a lime and wasn't sure if he liked the taste or not. "It doesn't make a hell of a lot of sense, but yeah, we read it."

"That's why I didn't tell you." The entry on Zach was unlike any other he'd ever seen. It still confused the hell out of him, and until he could do a bit more research he wasn't going to call his brother a witch. "Why aren't you two in the great room?"

They shivered.

"Mom's here?" Christopher raced from the room, ignoring the shouts of his brothers. He slid to a stop in the great room and found Zachary, hands holding what looked like a purple rose, standing over his end table and staring intently at the vase of flowers sitting there. Staring up at him was a tiny little old woman intoning, "You've got it. Now, cast."

Zachary's hand flew out. The rose touched the vase.

"At my touch this color you'll see. As I will so mote it be."

Christopher grinned. The flowers were turning a rich, deep purple. Not his favorite color, but if Grammy could help Zachary with his magic, he could live with the illusion of purple flowers for a bit.

Zachary whooped. "Yes!"

Christopher's grin slowly faded. The vase was turning purple. Then the end table. The lamp. The sofa.

The walls.

"Zachary. Take the illusion off." Purple bled across his hardwood floors. He stepped back, worried about what would happen if the leading edge touched him.

"Oops." Zachary turned to the elderly woman who stood there, shaking her head and pinching the bridge of her nose.

"I told you not to get overly excited." She sighed and waved her arm. Then she frowned. "Zachary."

"I'm trying!" Zachary leaned down and peered at the purple flowers. "Well. Crap."

"What?" Christopher was glad the purple stopped on the edge of the kitchen.

Zachary straightened up, his face filled with wonder. "It's not an illusion." He turned to Christopher, a huge grin slowly taking over his face. "It's not an illusion, Chris."

The wondrous happiness on Zach's face was something he hadn't seen since they were children. It made him sad to realize how much Zach's apparent lack of ability had dragged his happy-go-lucky brother down.

Chris blinked as his brother's words sank in. He got down on the ground and touched the floor, using all of his senses, magical and wolf, to detect the spell.

There *was* no spell. The lingering traces sifted over his senses, the faint hint of rose and lavender, but the spell was no longer active. "My great room is purple."

"Sorry." Zachary didn't sound very sorry. He sounded ecstatic. "I'll try and fix it."

"*No!*" Two strong voices rang out, one male, one female.

Christopher and Grammy looked at each other. The old woman laughed. "Zachary, you are to touch *nothing* until I've got you properly trained. Preferably under shields. And wards. Maybe even underground."

"I'm that bad?" Zachary tossed the rose onto the couch. "What am I saying? Of course I'm that bad." He started for the kitchen, his expression the same old devil-may-care Zachary Christopher was so used to seeing and was finally beginning to understand was a mask. "We need to make lunch. I'm starved."

"Zachary David Elijah Beckett."

There was power in the old woman's voice, enough power to stop Zachary in his tracks.

"Do you hereby swear to abide by the laws of the Witch's Council?"

Zachary turned to Annabelle, ignoring Christopher's gasp of surprise. "I do."

"Do you swear fealty to our Prince, forsaking all other oaths?"

Christopher swallowed. To swear fealty to the ruler of the Witches was to forswear his oath to the Wizards. It meant his baby brother would no longer be in the same Court as the rest of the family, would no longer answer to the Wizard King.

Zach took a deep breath and let it out slowly. "I do."

The woman smiled and winked. "One last oath."

Zachary smiled back. "Law of three."

One salt and pepper brow rose. "Very good." The smile dropped from her face and she was once more all business. "Do you promise to stand before our prince and swear your oath to him, binding yourself forevermore to Court and Council?"

Christopher frowned. That last part wasn't a part of the wizard's oath.

But Zachary showed no hesitation. "I do."

"I now pronounce you husband and wife! You may kiss the bride." Christopher turned to find Lana in the doorway, clapping her hands. "See, Grammy? Didn't I tell you?" Lana entered the room and gave Zachary a huge hug. "Congratulations!"

"Thanks." Zachary looked stunned. "What happens next?"

"You go for training, silly!" Lana turned to Annabelle, her arms still looped loosely around Zachary's neck. "Philadelphia?"

Grams shook her head. "Cleveland."

"The court? Already?"

Grams nodded.

"Whoa."

Zachary lifted his hands from Lana's waist, which was a very good thing. Christopher had been wondering how pissed his mom would be if Zachary came for Thanksgiving minus arms. "Wait wait wait. The court. Now?" He pulled out of Lana's arms and began pacing. "I know I have to swear fealty, but

205

shouldn't I have more training before going to court?"

Lana giggled. "Silly. The court will *be* your trainer." She waved her arm around at the purple great room. "This was supposed to be a simple illusion spell, right?"

Zach grimaced. "Right."

Annabelle smirked. "Be grateful I didn't ask you to change your eye color to purple. You'd look like Barney."

Christopher choked, covering his mouth with his hand.

Lana pointed at him. "I wouldn't laugh if I were you. Everyone associated with him could have looked like Grape Apes too." She blinked, her hand going to her neck. She turned to Zach, laughing. "No spells!"

Zach was looking down at his hands. "But I can't even cast a basic shield."

Annabelle patted Zach on the back. "Of course not. You've been learning from *wizards*." She smiled, and somehow Christopher was afraid. "By the time the court is done with you, shields should come easier than breathing. It'll be the other lessons you'll need to worry about." Grams turned her dark-eyed stare Christopher's way. "Now what is this about a duel?" She crossed her arms. "And how is my granddaughter involved?"

The doorbell rang before he could answer. "I'll get it!"

He ran for the front door, hearing the sounds of Zachary and Lana describing Cole's latest threats to her grandmother. Without looking through the peephole, he pulled open the door.

He nearly sobbed. Today just kept getting better and better. Edward and Marjory Beckett stood on his step, his mother cool and icy in her pale blue jacket, his father's salt and pepper hair rumpled as usual. "Hi, Mom. Dad."

His father paused long enough to give him a hug, his

golden eyes filled with anxiety. "Gareth?"

"My study."

His father rushed past him toward the study, barely acknowledging anyone else in his need to see his injured child.

"Christopher." His mother glided past him, pulling her light wool jacket off and handing it to him. "Where are your other brothers?"

He happily threw his brothers to the wolf. "Zachary is practicing some spells in the great room, and Daniel is with Gareth in my study."

She walked into the great room. "Zachary, you know better than to…" She stopped and slowly looked around. "Christopher, when did you redecorate?"

"Long story." He walked over to Lana and pulled her to him, tucking her under his shoulder. "Mom, I'd like you to meet Alannah and her grandmother, Mrs. Evans. Lana, Annabelle, this is my mother, Marjory Beckett."

His mother stiffened. "Annabelle Evans."

Grammy smiled, her gaze never leaving his mother. "Nice to meet you, Mrs. Beckett."

"Matriarch of the Evans coven?"

Annabelle's smile was full of teeth. If Chris didn't know any better he'd call *her* the predator. "The one and only."

His mother took a deep breath. "And Alannah is also an Evans, I presume?"

Christopher winced. "Evans-Beckett." Lana elbowed him in the side with a frown.

His mother turned, her frown equally dire. "Really?"

"Hello, Mrs. Beckett." Lana held out her hand with a smile.

His mother eyed the shadow mark on the side of her neck

and sighed. "A witch, Christopher?"

Lana's hand dropped, her eyes narrowing dangerously.

Uh-oh. "Alannah is my mate, Mother."

His mother waved her hand airily. "Don't call me Mother in that tone of voice. I've wiped your poopy bottom; I deserve at least some respect. Besides, I have no problems per se with witches. It's your father I'm worried about. You know how he gets." She sniffed. "Are you the one who turned Christopher's great room purple?"

"Um." Zach grinned weakly. "Is anyone hungry?"

"Zachary." She turned to Zachary, both brows in her hairline. Not a good sign. "What spell were you attempting?"

Zachary took a step away from his mother and closer to Annabelle. "I was trying an illusion spell on the flowers."

Mom blinked. "Illusion spell."

He nodded. "Yes."

"Goddess above, Zachary." It was said in the tone of voice mothers everywhere had, weary and sad and somehow still filled with affection.

Lana fingered the mark on her neck, the exact same mark Mrs. Beckett wore on *her* neck. "Trust me, it could have been worse. We could have been instant spokeswomen for Welch's grape juice."

Christopher buried his face in her hair and tried not to laugh when his mother rolled her eyes. He slowly pulled her out of the room and left Zachary to explain to their mother what was going on. He wasn't certain he wanted to be in the same room as them when she heard the news her baby boy was a witch.

Besides, if anyone could handle his mother, it would be Annabelle Evans. The two were either going to hate each other or love one another and he wasn't sure which prospect frightened him more.

"Chris?" His father was holding the door to the study open. "There's something you need to see."

He exchanged a worried look with Lana before moving into the study. "What?"

Daniel turned The Registry around and pointed to a single entry. "Cole."

He read the entry and sucked in a breath. Why in hell was he so surprised? "That explains a lot."

Lana was frowning. "I thought you told me he was a wizard."

"He *was* a wizard once upon a time." Christopher shook his head. "Enough hatred can send a man down a path no one could predict."

She was shaking her head. "But that's supposed to be impossible. No one can go from wizard to warlock."

"Not true. They can if they already had some warlock blood in them." Daniel turned the book around. "See here? The Godwins have an ancestor who married a warlock, two generations before our families intermarried."

Chris felt like he'd been socked in the jaw. "Does that mean what I think it means?"

His father nodded. "There's a direct line down from their ancestor to the one who married ours." He braced himself on the desk. "It means a warlock could also be born into the Becketts."

"Fuck." Gareth sat gingerly in the chair behind the desk. "So where's the witch in the family? I mean, how did Zach wind up one?"

Lana shook her head. "Witches are spontaneous,

remember? We tend to show up in the same families over and over again, but sometimes a witch is born into a wizard or warlock family and, unless someone picks up on it or checks The Registry, they never know who or what they really are. Sometimes we find them and try to train them, but how well they do depends on how much they're willing to accept."

"We have another problem than Zach's spontaneous witchdom." Daniel stared at Chris, his expression grim.

Chris nodded. "We've been preparing for a wizard."

"When we should have been preparing for a warlock." Lana parked her butt on the edge of his work table, her fingers automatically going to the emerald ring. She toyed with it before slipping it absently onto her finger. Chris tried to focus on the problem at hand rather than what she'd just done. "We need to get Grammy and your mom in here."

"I agree." His brothers looked at him like he'd just offered to share office space with Jaws and the Terminator, but his father looked oddly pleased. "We also need to let the court know Cole is no longer a wizard, and therefore no longer eligible for the role of king."

"I'll take care of that." Daniel picked up the phone and began dialing.

"I'll get Mom, Annabelle and Zach." Gareth pulled himself wearily to his feet. "These fucking pain pills are really dragging my ass down."

"Rest after this." When Gareth opened his mouth to object, Chris held up his hand, silencing him. "You can help me more when you're at the top of your game. Take a nap, then come back down and help me prepare for my duel."

Gareth nodded and dragged himself out of the room.

"Chris?"

He looked down into the worried eyes of his mate. "It will be all right, Lana." He pressed a kiss to those soft, beautiful lips. "I promise."

She glared up at him, but he saw the worry dragging at her eyes. "It better be."

He smiled. He knew what he'd be dealing with during the duel, could prepare for what a warlock might throw at him.

He was positive he'd be able to keep his promise.

Chapter Twenty

"So what's the plan? Has he contacted you yet with a location? A date, a time?"

Lana watched the Beckett boys get serious in Chris's workroom. Gareth was busy thumbing through Chris's spell books, awkwardly leaving little sticky tabs to mark pages with his good hand.

Daniel was polishing Chris's athame, a magical knife used by all three types of magic users. Spells could be channeled through an athame in much the same way as a wand.

Edward, their father, was quietly consulting with someone on the phone about binding spells.

Zachary was muttering to himself, closing his eyes and running words around in his head. She could hear the beginnings of rhymes, chants to cast spells on items to help Chris protect himself. Every now and then he would stop and scribble something down, his full lip caught between his teeth. Sometimes his hand would reach out absently and snag something, running it around and around his fingers before either adding it to his pile or setting it aside. Whenever he reached for something, his brothers would watch him with various degrees of amusement and wonder.

She didn't have the heart to tell Zach that a witch's spells wouldn't work very well for a wizard.

Then again, considering everything else he'd accomplished, perhaps his *would*. It was something to think about, anyway.

She, on the other hand, had been relegated to kitchen help. She was bringing the men coffee and sandwiches while they worked, and while it rankled she sort of understood. Just watching the precise way they worked, the way Christopher would lay out different things, study them, put most of them away and set one aside, showed her she wouldn't have much to contribute. It was like he was building a beautiful mosaic, once piece at a time, and she wouldn't be able to see his vision until after he'd finished.

It was so goddamn sexy. It was the same focus he had when they made love, the fierce concentration making her think wicked thoughts.

Made love. Lana smiled. She didn't know what it was about the arrogant wolf and his family, but she felt like she'd come home.

She handed him his sandwich and coffee, returning the absent smile he gave her. He pushed his glasses up his nose and bent to study the talisman currently sitting on his desk, strange runes she'd never seen before etched on its surface. "What is that?"

"Protection amulet," he responded absently. "Need it for a shielding spell."

She stroked it, feeling the dormant magic within it. "Groovy."

His lips twitched. He looked up at her over the top of his glasses. "Groovy?"

She shrugged. "Isn't that what Shaggy always says?"

He shook his head, pinching the bridge of his nose under his glasses, but she could see the way his mouth trembled from trying to hold in the laugh.

Next thing she knew Chris tumbled her into his lap. She squeaked, grabbing hold of his shoulders. He nipped her chin. "Who gets to be Thelma?"

"Not me!" Zach held up his hand, grinning, still writing scribbles on pieces of paper.

Lana tapped her lips with her fingernail, getting into the game. She could sense some of the tension leaving their shoulders. "You're more Danger-Prone Daphne, I think."

Zach sputtered indignantly while his brothers laughed.

Chris leaned down and kissed the tip of her nose. "Daniel would make an interesting Thelma."

"And Gareth could be Fred, since he leads your merry little band of misfits."

Chris grinned. "He *has* pulled Zachary's ass out of the fire more than once."

Lana nodded, her own lips turning up. "And Zach does have a real fondness for the color purple."

Gareth was leaning against a bookcase, face buried in his arm, his shoulders shaking. Daniel was openly grinning at his brother Zach.

"Oh fuck you all." Zach stood up and stretched. "I'm going to get some chips." He strode out, but not before flipping his brothers off.

"I knew you were trouble." Chris gave her a soft kiss. "Thank you for the sandwiches."

"You're welcome." She climbed off his lap. "I'll let you boring types get back to work." She sauntered out of the office, grinning. She found Zach in the kitchen. "Hey, Daphne."

"Hey, Shaggy."

"Are those barbeque?" She reached for the bag.

He held it over his head. "Get your own."

214

Lana stuck her tongue out at him. "You know there isn't much we can do to help them, right?"

He lowered the bag to the counter with a sigh. "Yeah, I know."

"There's still stuff we *can* do."

He crinkled the top of the bag. "Like bring them chips?" He looked so lost, like a kicked puppy. She just wanted to cuddle him, but she didn't think Chris would appreciate finding her stroking his brother's head.

"Do you really think Cole is going to fight fair?"

He paused. "He has to. There are certain rules to wizard duels that must be adhered to. If they aren't, the duel is automatically won by the wizard who did follow the rules."

She settled onto one of the counter stools and propped her chin in her hand. "But Cole isn't a wizard."

"True." He popped a chip in his mouth, but she could practically hear him thinking things through.

She kicked her foot back and forth, fighting the urge to pace. "What are the odds he'll cheat somehow?"

"Not sure. I don't know him the way Christopher does."

She had to know. The thought of it was driving her insane. "Is this a duel to the death?"

Zach stopped popping chips in his mouth. "Death?" He swallowed. "There have been very few wizard duels ending in death."

"Yeah, but Cole wants Christopher to hurt, remember? So could he make it a duel to the death?" She picked up another chip. "Actually, a better question would be *would* he?"

Zach frowned, and she caught a glimpse in his determined expression of the kind of witch he would be when his training was over. *Man, the court is going to have an interesting time with him.* "No. Damn it, he wouldn't." He grabbed her hand and dragged her into the workroom. "Chris, we need an extra protection amulet."

"Why?"

"Do you really think he'll leave Lana out of this?"

Chris froze. "The duel is between him and me. Lana will have no part in it. Besides, she's already wearing a protection amulet."

"Your *strongest* amulet? Besides, who said it would have anything to do with the duel?"

Chris's head rose. Zach just stood there, clenching Lana's hand in one of his own, the other held out for the amulet he'd demanded. "Zach?"

"I have a *very bad feeling*, Chris. Give me the amulet."

Lana's eyes widened. "Give him the amulet." If Zach's instincts were screaming at him *that* loudly then she knew she'd need whatever it was he was planning on doing.

Chris held out the amulet. "If he goes after her, he'll be expecting wizard's magic."

"And a witch's. Remember, he knows what Lana is. He'll be anticipating she'll protect herself. And if she doesn't he'd have to know Annabelle sure as hell would." Daniel propped his butt on the edge of Chris's desk.

Zach smiled. It was feral, cold, and nothing Lana would have thought him capable of. From the looks on his brothers' faces, they never would have either. "But that's where we'll have an edge. He won't be expecting *me*."

Chris stared at his brother for the longest moment before an identical smile crossed his face. Lana shivered. "Good."

Zach turned, dragging Lana out of the room behind him. "Zach?"

"Trust me."

She blew her hair out of her eyes. *What are you planning, Zach?* She watched him frantically lay out items on the kitchen counter, his expression hard and his movements precise and controlled. He knew exactly what he wanted and where to find it. The more she watched, the more it made sense. And the more it made sense, the more frightened she became. He needed to get to court and he needed to get there *soon.*

If Zach is capable of this, what else is he capable of?

Chapter Twenty-One

The chamber door clanged shut with an ominous sound. How Cole had managed to obtain a dueling chamber on such short notice Christopher didn't know. He had the feeling he'd used his family connections to cut through the red tape.

The Godwins sat on Cole's side of the chamber, glaring at the Becketts through cold eyes. In particular Lana and Annabelle Evans seemed to be garnering the most attention. Arthur Godwin, Cole's brother, had a particularly vile expression on his face when he saw the mark on Lana's neck, the unmistakable stamp of a Beckett mate.

It was a typical dueling ring, a simple white ring like you'd see in a circus, perhaps. But where the circle of a circus ring would be plain white bags or pavers, this white ring was etched with arcane symbols in all sorts of colors, the markings necessary not only for the shielding spell that would encase them once the duel started but full of protection spells designed to make sure those outside the ring would suffer no ill effects from whatever magic the duelists utilized. Instead of grandstands there were comfortable padded chairs opposite one another, enough to hold the members of each family plus a few extras. Since neither Cole nor Christopher had called anyone but family, some of those chairs on each side remained empty. The floor of the circle itself was simple dirt, earth necessary to ground certain spells or to be used against your opponent in whatever way you could. A water fountain gurgled nearby. A chimenea already had a fire burning merrily inside. Incense scented the air directly above the dueling ring, the burner hanging by a golden chain. These items allowed elemental magic to be used once the shields snapped into place.

Christopher stared at his opponent, mentally checking each and every one of his preparations. Two amulets, a piece of paper with a specific rune in gold lettering, a silver lighter, a stick figure, black ribbon, three round silver links attached to each other, and his Athame. Not much on the surface, but each one had a purpose. He couldn't, wouldn't turn and look at his family or his mate until after this little fight was over. He needed to concentrate solely on kicking Cole's ass so hard he'd feel it in the afterlife. This stupid rivalry had to end.

He planned on ending it tonight.

He'd already hashed all of the details out with Gareth, who had agreed to be his second. Together they'd found a way a man could take the power of another being and bind it in such a way that the person could never again do harm to others. It was an old spell, rarely used by any but the council's Enforcers, and could wind up costing Christopher more than it cost Cole. But if it meant keeping Lana safe, Christopher would risk it. Cole was a menace. He needed to be dealt with. Cole's willingness to harm innocents in his little war with Christopher just cemented Chris's resolve.

He risked one quick glance at Cole's second, the man's father, and wondered what he thought of the duel. Did he know why Cole was fighting Christopher? Did he approve of it?

Did he know what his son had become?

The cold gleam in the man's eyes, the pure satisfaction and vindictiveness there, told him Cole's father was just as deeply into this madness as Cole was. He wished he'd looked up the entire Godwin family just to see who else in this room was a warlock.

The Arbiter, the wizard responsible for ensuring a fair duel, paced off the length of the dueling area, surrounding them in a shimmering, barely visible shield. It would effectively prevent either the Becketts or the Godwins from assisting their relatives, making sure the duel remained strictly between the two combatants. No outside interference would be allowed.

Inside the shield, however, a wizard could use any means at his disposal to defeat his opponent. Only the seconds would be able to enter the ring, and only under specific circumstances.

To be on the safe side, Zachary had informed the Arbiter before anyone entered the arena that Chris was not dealing with a wizard, but with a warlock. The Arbiter had made the appropriate adjustments to the circle.

Or so Chris hoped.

"Mr. Beckett. Mr. Godwin. Are you both intent on this duel?" The deep voice of the Arbiter startled him, breaking his thoughts.

"Yes," Cole hissed.

"Yes." Christopher shook his head. He had to be one hundred percent on his guard. He couldn't afford to be distracted, not even by his thoughts.

The shield closed, sealing them inside. Only the Arbiter could break it.

Or the Arbiter's death, but Christopher didn't think even the Godwins would go *that* far. Killing an Arbiter was considered worse than cheating in a duel, the punishments far more severe.

The Arbiter lowered his arms and nodded. The duel was officially on.

Now. Christopher pulled out his athame and began his chant, fingering his protection charm. Cole, not surprisingly, mirrored his actions.

Yet something was off about the other man's magic. Christopher could sense the forces coalescing around Cole, but there was a taint to his magic that hadn't been there the last time he'd faced Cole.

Christopher began his chant, hoping for the best.

"Lord and Lady, come to me.

Protect me from adversity."

He pointed the athame at Cole.

"Any ill you send to me

Will return to you times three.

As I will so mote it be!"

He finished his protection spell and felt it settle into his skin. It would be harder to hurt him now, but not impossible. Every protection spell had a weakness. All it would take would be for Cole to figure out his weakness and he'd be able to harm Christopher.

But it did buy him time. Christopher pulled out the second amulet, watching Cole closely. Cole pulled out a wand of dark wood, his gaze full of hate.

The tainted magic struck before Christopher could even start his chant. It struck him in the middle of his chest, pulling at the core of his being. He could feel it burning into him with icy-hot talons. He gasped, desperately trying to get his breath. He tossed the three silver links to the ground.

"Circle three I conjure thee.

Ground his spell so mote it be!"

He drew in a desperate breath, grateful when Cole's spell was jerked into the rings. The rings expanded, digging into the earth of the dueling circle, grounding both Christopher and Cole's spell. He touched the edge of the burn on his chest and hissed. He knew the throbbing pain would only grow worse, a distraction he didn't need.

He needed to end this duel quickly, before the pain made him mess up one of his spells. If that happened, he would lose everything he was fighting for.

Cole ground his teeth and put his wand, now useless, away. "Clever, Christopher. Try this one on for size." He tossed a reddish gold circlet on the ground and leveled his athame at it. The blade danced with a sickly green light.

"By Lucifer's might and Lilith's hate

I conjure thee, come through the gate."

Christopher didn't wait to hear more. He moved to counteract the spell. He took out the second amulet. He had intended to use it to hold off whatever elemental forces Cole had chosen to conjure. Instead, the man had chosen to conjure a demon. He tossed the amulet to the ground.

"Thrice around the circle's bound

Sink all evil to the ground!"

He drew three circles around the amulet with his athame and began pouring his power into it, hoping it would be enough to hold whatever would come through the slowly building gate.

Chapter Twenty-Two

Lana couldn't believe what she was witnessing. "He's summoning a fucking demon." She turned to the Becketts. "Is that fucking legal?"

"No." Edward Beckett stood, glaring at the Arbiter. "Open the damn shield."

The Arbiter grimaced, his hands waving. "I can't. I'm being blocked."

A low growl sounded from behind her. She turned to see Daniel, eyes glowing eerily, staring at the Godwin family across the barrier. Next to him his father, Edward Beckett, was beginning to remove his clothing. "Oh boy." She couldn't even appreciate the view of the male Becketts disrobing. Chris was in danger, and it was all she could focus on.

When Zach pulled her away from the Becketts she went willingly, especially since he was dragging her toward the barrier.

Cole grinned at Christopher. He pricked his finger with his burning athame and allowed three drops to land in the dirt inside the reddish gold circlet. *Fuck. A conjuration using blood? I am screwed.*

"Bound by blood, obey my call

Holding demon's might in thrall."

And where was the Arbiter? Once Cole began conjuring a demon he should have taken down the shield and declared the duel null and void, since it was obvious Cole was cheating. No outside help was supposed to enter the circle. Only elemental spells were allowed, and not even summoning spells. No salamanders, no water sprites, none of them should be able to enter the circle. And how the fuck was he doing this, anyway? Christopher could feel the tendrils of the summoning sinking into the earth, seeking to pull something twisted and dark into their realm.

He had to stop this before Cole finished his chant, or he wouldn't be the only one to suffer. No demon would want to stop with just Christopher's blood. It would want the entire family.

He pulled out the stick figure and the black ribbon, ignoring the vicious pain stabbing into him. It pulsed in time with the tendrils of the conjuring circle, scaring the crap out of him. He'd been injured by demonic magic. It would take one hell of a spell to heal him completely. If it proved resistant to white magic he'd be in agony for the rest of his life.

Christopher stood. Cole would never harm another being, never threaten Lana again. He strode over to Cole's conjuring circle and dipped the stick figure in the drop of blood. "Big mistake, Cole. Huge."

Cole licked his lips nervously. Christopher ignored the warlock and began to bind the stick figure with the black ribbon.

Cole continued his chant, his expression full of panicky determination.

"By the Compact take your toll

Feast upon this gifted soul."

Cole pulled out his own doll. There, tied to its middle, was a small piece of fur.

Wolf fur.

Crap. I am definitely screwed.

Lana ignored the two wolves streaking past her. "Concentrate on the barrier. We have to take it down, have to get to Chris."

"Right." Zach took a deep breath and placed his palm against the barrier. "I have to figure out how it was cast. I...I have to find the grounding."

Lana grabbed him. "Stop thinking like a wizard and start thinking like a witch!"

He turned to her, his eyes blank from shock. "Think like a witch." He blinked, his eyes refocusing, his gaze centering on the shield. His expression became cold and certain. "No. Not wizard, not witch." He stepped back and raised his arms. Power arched between his hands, glowing above him, clean and pure, a powerful counterpoint to the rancid energies behind the barrier. "Me."

Lana felt her jaw hit the floor as Zach's magic, pure white and damn near blinding, blasted into the barrier.

What. The. Fuck? She'd *never* seen anything like that before.

This family was just *full* of surprises.

Christopher watched the swirling green and black mist widen in the golden circlet, a dark evil presence making itself felt in his very bones. *Oh fuck.* He began the binding chant, praying to the gods he was in time. He wound the black ribbon around the Cole doll.

"I bind thee three times three."

He wound the ribbon again.

"By this charm do no more harm."

He wrapped the ribbon one last time, making sure to touch the tiny spot of Cole's blood on the top of the figure.

"I bind you, Cole, your blood, your soul!"

But he was too late. Before he could tie off the ends of the ribbon and finish the spell, Cole screamed the last bit of *his* spell.

"By your oath you will obey.

Demon come forth and claim your prey!"

But Christopher didn't stop. He couldn't. If that *thing* got out, it would spell the end of himself, his family and Lana. He tied off the ends of the binding spell and finished the chant.

"By air and earth, water and fire

So be you bound with no more power.

Lord and Lady, hear my plea.

As I will so mote it be!"

Christopher tossed the Cole doll into the widening demonic circle and prayed.

The sudden silence was deafening. "No." Cole's horrified whisper matched his expression. The doll slowly sank into the inky darkness. "What have you done?"

"Oh shit." Zach's face clenched in pain, his hands closing. He pulled the power back into himself. The barrier was still intact, but there were signs of his assault. Some of the protection runes had dimmed. "He's screwed."

Lana turned and saw Christopher toss the doll into the

black maw at his feet. She felt her heart stop beating. "Chris."
She dropped to her knees. She couldn't lose him. How could
she lose him? She'd just found him. *"Chris!"*

"No!"

Cole's last word trailed off into a terrified scream. A dark,
inhuman arm appeared out of the hole, grasping Cole's ankle in
a blackened grip. Cole gasped, his eyes going wide, his face
strangely blanked.

Then the arm *pulled,* but it didn't pull Cole. A stream of
dark energy poured out from Cole, whisking away into the dark
opening, draining away until the warlock collapsed. Then the
arm went back to where it had come from, the demon hole
closing behind it until no hint was left that it had ever been
there. Other than the blackened, broken ring of gold and a
small spot of darkness in the earth, nothing remained of the
demon's presence.

Cole didn't move. Christopher knelt down and checked his
pulse.

Cole's body was burning cold. Christopher lifted his hand
away rapidly, blowing on the tips of his fingers. He wasn't
certain but he might have left some flesh behind. He looked
toward the Arbiter, who stood there in visible shock. "He's
dead."

The Arbiter raised his arms. This time, the shields obeyed
him and fell with nary a sound.

Once the shield was down, Lana was in the circle, running
toward Christopher. He waited for her, pulling her to him
carefully, ignoring the continuing battle between the remaining
Godwins, the Becketts and the Arbiter. He focused instead on
the shaking woman in his arms, holding her as tight to him as
he dared, reassuring himself she was unharmed. Her hands

roamed over his chest, her tears falling on the burn marks. Zach's bad feeling had centered around Lana, *not* Christopher. How had things gone so horribly wrong?

"Chris! Look out!"

He turned at the sound of Zach's voice. Davis Godwin, Cole's father, held his son's blackened wand in his hands. Green fire began pouring forth. He barely moved in time to keep Lana from taking the brunt of the spell. Weakened already by Cole's previous blast, he fell, dragging her down with him, the pain boring into his side in unending, icy agony.

"You killed my son!" Davis stood over Christopher, ignoring the battle still raging behind him. He tried to finish the job Cole had started. His face was set in a rictus of hate.

Suddenly Zach was there, a glow around him Christopher had never seen before. The green fire met the glowing barrier around his brother and bounced onto Davis, striking the wand. With a shriek of rage, he dropped it just before it exploded.

Zach pointed his finger at Davis. "Back the fuck off, warlock." He flicked his finger, and the man flew backward, landing with a hard thud against the side of the building. He fell in a graceless heap and didn't get move again.

Zach bent over Christopher, the glow still surrounding him. "You okay, bro?"

Christopher tried to stand but found he couldn't. He hissed in pain, his side protesting the movement viciously. He was just too injured. "No."

Lana pushed him over, ignoring his indrawn scream. She bent and examined his new wound. "It's bad, Zach."

Christopher looked down and saw the blackened flesh, the blisters already broken and wet. He could feel the taint under his skin and knew the Godwins had won.

Christopher didn't hear his brother's response. All he saw was Lana bending over him, tears in those pretty eyes of hers. "Hey."

She sniffled. "Hey yourself, wolfman."

He could feel the darkness tugging at him. "Don't go."

She sobbed. "Not going anywhere. You hear me? Chris?"

His world turned black, his last sight the one he had hoped to see when he lay down in the dark forever.

"Chris?" She watched his golden eyes close, his breathing shallow and uneven. They needed to get him some help, more than she could provide. Blood was beginning to puddle beneath him. If he bled too much more it would take a miracle to save him.

"Help me." She looked up to find Zach holding out his hand. His other pressed into the wound in Chris's side. Tears filled his eyes. "One hand in mine, one on the ground. Please, Lana. Trust me. Complete the circle."

Complete the... Oh. *Oh!* This was what Zach had worked so hard on in the kitchen the day before. He'd done something to the protection amulet, something she barely grasped. She took out the amulet and held it in her hand, placing it between Zach's palm and her own. She slapped the other against the earth and opened herself up to Zach's magic and Chris's life force. The mark of the wolf throbbed on her neck in response, pulsing in time to Chris's weakening heartbeat. Her instincts told her what Zach had planned was going to hurt like hell, but if it worked, it would be more than worth it. She focused on Chris's face and waited for the pain to hit, knowing the amulet should block at least some of it.

Zach closed his eyes and began to chant, the words lilting and strange. Agony seared through her, more than she'd thought a person could endure and live. She couldn't hear the words Zach spoke.

After a few more minutes, she couldn't even hear her own screams.

Chapter Twenty-Three

Chris faced off with his brother Zach, fury pounding in his veins. "I should kill you."

Zach rubbed one of his hands wearily over his face. The other was swathed in bandages. Zach refused to allow him to see it without them. "She's alive, Chris. So are you." He shrugged. "If I hadn't done what I did, you would have been lost."

"But she would be alive."

"She still *is* alive, bro. Believe it or not, she'll be fine."

Chris growled. He was holding his wolf back with everything in him, but it was close. Zach had put his mate in mortal danger to save him, and Chris was furious. Somehow Zach had taken the hellish wounds from him, grounding the evil power *through* Lana, cleansing it before allowing it to return to the earth. Because of Zach, Lana had suffered horror before finally blacking out. She'd been unconscious ever since.

Zach deserved at least a beating for putting causing Lana to suffer. "If you hadn't done what you did, she wouldn't be lying half dead in my bed right now."

Zach glared at him, power sparkling in his eyes. "If I hadn't done what I did, *you would be dead.* Lana would be alone. Fuck, Chris! Some of the Godwins are still fucking out there. What did you expect me to do? Let you die?"

That was the only reason he'd been able to keep himself from attacking Zach. He could almost understand what had driven Zach to torture his mate. He wasn't quite certain he wouldn't have tried to do something similar if it had been Zach lying on the ground, Zach's life force slowly leeching away.

Not that he understood exactly what Zach had done. None of them did. The scariest part was the fear Annabelle tried to hide when she looked at her new protégé. Zach was turning into something none of them had ever encountered before, something capable of facing a demonic spell and winning.

Still... "If Lana had died, you would have lost me anyway."

Zach growled. "Lana was not going to die."

"She might have."

The weird glow was once more surrounding his baby brother, and it was beginning to scare the shit out of him. "I wouldn't have allowed it." Zach took a deep breath, and the glow died down. "Trust me, Chris." Zach turned away and headed for his room. "For once in our lives just...believe in me."

Chris watched his brother walk up the stairs, his heart hurting at the defeat in his brother's face but unable to give up his anger. He would, given time. Zach was right; Lana was still alive, and that was what he needed to focus on.

"I won't kill him, but I'm still going to fucking kick his ass."

Lana felt the darkness receding, Chris's voice rolling over her in a furious wave. *Uh-oh. Wonder who pissed Chris off.* Her head pounded, and her mouth felt like she hadn't had anything to drink in days.

Gareth's voice was low and soothing. "You can't kick his ass if he's in Cleveland, Christopher."

Who's going to Cleveland? She tried to turn her head, but

the pain was too intense. What the hell had she been drinking? This was the worst hangover in the history of drunkenness!

"I don't care. I'll figure out a way to do it. How dare he use her to save me?" It sounded like Chris was pacing. *But Chris never paces.* She frowned. *Wait. Who used me? And for what?*

"Stop being a shithead about this. You would have *died*, Chris."

"So?"

"She volunteered."

"I don't fucking care. Zach should have found another way to ground the spell. Hell, he could have grounded it through me."

"Christopher." She could hear Gareth's frustrated sigh and wondered how long they'd been fighting. "Grounding it through you wasn't an option. You *know* that. You were part of the spell, not the solution."

It was starting to come back to her. Chris had been lying on the ground, bleeding badly. Cole's body had been close by, eerily still. The Godwins had been fighting the Becketts while the Arbiter tried to stop it all and failed miserably.

"He could have asked someone else."

"We were all dealing with the Godwins. Damn it, Chris! Zach had seconds to act. If he'd waited for one of us, you'd be dead."

Oh. Zach. That picture was probably going to stick with her forever. Zach kneeling over Chris's body, glowing and holding out his hand, begging for her help. At the thought of the new witch, Lana winced. The spell he'd used, forcing the toxins from the wound through her, purifying them before grounding them, had been excruciating. But with no time to come up with an alternative way it had been the *only* way to save Chris from the wound rapidly killing him. Cleansing the taint before releasing it into the ground meant no one else would suffer ill effects from the demonic power. Otherwise the clean earth of the dueling circle would have been twisted and perverted, unable to sustain the spells of the wizards who used it.

The power Cole Godwin had held was apparently nothing compared to what Davis Godwin had. The second wound had been more horrific than the first. *Thank the Lord and Lady the wand was destroyed.* She'd hate to think what would happen if an object of such evil was ever placed in the hands of someone even stronger than Davis Godwin.

She shifted her leg, hoping in some weird way it would alleviate the pain in her head. That's when she realized it wasn't just her head hurting. Her whole body did.

"I think she's waking up." A hand gently picked up hers, even the soft touch painful. "Sweetheart?"

"Ow." She hoped he'd heard her, because the barely there whisper was the best she could do.

"Get Annabelle. *Now.*"

The authority in his hushed voice was reassuring. She felt her lips curl up at the thought of her mate being his usual bossy self.

"I don't know what you're smiling about, sweetheart. The minute Annabelle gives you a clean bill of health I'm spanking your ass so hard you won't sit down for a week." He stroked her hair away from her face. She thought it trembled. "I still can't believe you and Zach did that."

She couldn't really speak, couldn't move without wanting to scream, so she did the only thing she could. She pursed her lips and blew him a kiss.

His breath caught. "Fuck it." She felt the bed dip. "Annabelle can kiss my ass."

If she had the strength, she would have giggled.

"I know it hurts, so I'm not going to try and hold you." His hand came to rest against her stomach. "But I can sure as hell *touch* you."

She licked her lips. "'Kay." It did hurt a little, but there was no way she'd tell him. They both needed to feel each other, to know everything was going to be okay.

She felt his lips press against her arm. "Go to sleep, sweetheart. I'll be here when you wake."

"Mm." She drifted off, trusting him to keep his word.

Christopher stared down at the woman sleeping in his bed. She hadn't opened her eyes once, barely spoke, and he'd never been more relieved in his life. She'd been out for two hellish days, days in which his baby brother had been whisked out of the house to face possible punishment for going against the wishes of Annabelle Evans, casting spells when she'd expressly forbidden it. He had the feeling the punishment would be more severe considering the cost to her granddaughter.

He yawned, weary beyond belief. He'd barely slept since they carried Lana into his bedroom, too afraid she'd wake up and he wouldn't be there.

Lana looked horrible. Her eyes were sunken, her skin sallow, her hair limp. If he didn't know better, he'd swear she suffered from a life-threatening illness. Her palm was bandaged, hiding the damage the protection amulet had done to her. He'd wanted to see the damage but Annabelle had told him to leave the bandages in place. The only good thing he could see was that her hand wasn't swathed the same way Zach's had been.

And she'd done this for him. He still couldn't quite get over it.

He'd have to make sure certain things were clear to her from now on. First off, he was never letting her out of his sight again. Second, she was to stay away from his insane brother. She and Zachary were a deadly combination. Third, he'd have to make sure she understood exactly what she meant to him.

In the meantime, he'd wait. When she woke, he'd be there. There was nowhere else he'd rather be.

"How is she?"

He turned his head slightly, careful not to jar his mate. "Sleeping again."

Annabelle frowned and studied Lana through narrowed eyes. "Let's take a look at her." She waved a hand at him. "Off the bed."

"No."

She glared at him. He glared right back, making sure his hand stayed relaxed against Lana's stomach. "I told you not to jar her at all. We're still not certain of the full effects of the spell Zach used."

"I was careful." He kept his voice low, but couldn't keep the warning out of his voice. His wolf was still howling in grief at the damage done to their mate. "We need to be here."

She cocked her hip, reminding him forcibly of the woman lying beside him. "Oh? *We?*"

He had no intention of getting into how the Beckett family curse worked with her. Annabelle Evans might be a powerful witch, but he was a wolf with an injured mate. There was no way in hell he was getting off the bed. "Do your examination."

She bristled at his commanding tone before huffing out a breath. "Wizards. Always have to have things your way." She bent over her granddaughter and began her careful examination.

Christopher watched, keeping a close eye on Annabelle. Her expression slowly eased, and so did the clamp around his heart.

When Annabelle smiled at him, he sighed in relief. Lana was going to be all right. "You look exhausted. As long as you don't jar her too much it should be safe for you to sleep there." She smoothed his hair from his forehead, much like his own grandmother had done when he was a child.

"Annabelle?"

"Hmm?"

"Thank you."

She nodded. "You're welcome."

The door shut quietly behind her, and Chris followed her advice. For the first time in two days he allowed himself to fall asleep.

Something woke him later in the day.

"Chris?"

"Mm."

"Chris."

He opened his eyes to darkness. "Still sleepin'."

A soft sigh blew across his hair. "Chris."

"What?"

"I'm thirsty."

He stifled a yawn. "M'kay." He turned on the bedside lamp and stumbled to the bathroom. Grabbing a cup he filled it with water and headed to the bed. "Here."

She blinked up at him. "Help me?"

"Mm." He took her into his arms and held the cup to her lips, her gasp of pain bringing him fully awake. "Oh crap. I'm sorry, little witch."

She took a sip of the water and settled in against him. "It's okay." She shuddered, her face pale and drawn. "Everything hurts."

"I have some ibuprofen Annabelle left for you in case you woke up, but she said you need to take it with food."

She grinned up weakly at him. "I'll wait while you fetch something."

One brow rose. "Fetch?"

"Go, boy! Go!"

He shook his head at her. "How can you be making jokes right now?"

"We won." Her bandaged hand caressed his cheek. "We're here, and Cole isn't."

"But his family got away." In the scramble to save Chris, the rest of the Godwins had gotten away. He wasn't certain what punishments the other family would receive but one thing was certain. The Godwins were out of the running for king as far as the court of the wizard king was concerned.

It had slipped *everyone's* attention that Cole and his family were actually warlocks. It had several of the wizard court's sages scratching their heads in disbelief. The entries into The Registry were clear, yet no one had thought to check until Gareth had started wondering exactly who Cole was working with. Once he'd pointed the entry out to Daniel, it was as if a veil was lifted from their eyes.

There were rumors that the Godwins would suffer no consequences other than formal expulsion from the wizard's court for all of their warlock family members. What Davis Godwin would do from there, Christopher didn't know, but he had the feeling this wasn't over. With Cole's death, the war between the Becketts and the Godwins had reached a new level.

"So you think it isn't over?" She snuggled against him with a wince.

"No. I don't. I'm sorry, little witch. I never meant to drag you into something like this."

She shot him a disgusted look. "Yup, you just grabbed hold of my arm and pasted a sign on my ass that said 'Warlocks Eat Free'." He growled. She giggled, then gasped. "Oh, remind me not to laugh."

"I'll go grab a snack for both of us. You settle down and try to rest." He placed a kiss on her forehead before heading for the kitchen.

A light was already on. "Hey, Gareth."

"Chris. How's Lana?"

Chris frowned when Gareth adjusted his sling. His older brother was in pain but ever since the fight with the Godwins he'd refused to take any of his medications. He said he didn't want his brain fuzzed if he had to wolf out. "She's hungry and wants some ibuprofen. She's in a lot of pain, but at least she's talking to me now and her eyes are open." He reached into the fridge and pulled out some cheese and grapes, hoping they'd be easy on her stomach.

"It's good she's awake." Gareth spooned up some chocolate ice cream and reached for the chocolate syrup on the counter. "We're looking further into how the Godwins managed to tamper with their entry into The Registry."

"We?"

Gareth started to shrug but stopped. "Daniel and I." Gareth stirred his ice cream and chocolate syrup together, making a sort of milkshake in his bowl. He'd been doing it since he was a child. "I think Daniel's going to want the ring soon."

Chris blinked. "Why?"

"Have you noticed how remote he's become?"

"He's always been a little aloof." He thought back to Daniel's recent behavior, the way he seemed to have closed himself off. "He's been worse?"

"He's holed up in his office or his house all the time now. He doesn't leave except for family stuff like this."

Sounds familiar. Poor bastard. He'd done the same thing before going to his father and begging him for the ring. "I'll talk to him, let him know the ring will be ready for him as soon as he needs it."

The only problem was, Lana loved the family ring. He'd have to explain to her how it belonged to all the Becketts, not just him.

But it did give him ideas on what sort of engagement ring he'd buy for Lana. Perhaps he'd replace the family emerald with another one. He liked the look of Venus's stone on her hand.

Besides, now that she wore his mark, she no longer needed the ring. It would pass on to the next Beckett who was ready to find his mate.

"Chris?"

"Yeah?"

"He told me earlier he's thinking about transferring to Philadelphia."

Chris finished loading the tray with two glasses of milk. "Really?"

He picked up the tray and turned to find Gareth studying him closely. "You don't sound surprised."

Chris laughed wearily. "First off, I think I've used up all my surprise for the next month or so. Second..." Chris shook his head and headed out of the kitchen. "I don't know. Something tells me it would be the right move."

Gareth followed him up the stairs. "Isn't it Lana's job to go on instinct?"

Chris snorted. "Open the door for me."

Gareth opened the bedroom door, but stopped Chris with a hand on his arm. "Hey."

"What?" At this point Chris just wanted to crawl into bed with his mate.

"They did the right thing."

"Who?"

"Lana and Zach."

Chris growled.

"You don't know what it did to Zach, Chris."

He stopped growling. "You do?"

Gareth grimaced. "Let's just say I don't think he'll ever be the same." The sorrow on Gareth's face had Chris rethinking a few things. "Just don't be too hard on him the next time you see him."

Chris nodded and, satisfied, Gareth let him go. "Good night, Chris."

"Night, Gareth." He entered the bedroom and pushed the door closed with his foot. Lana was watching him with a frown. "What?"

"Did you give Zach a hard time?"

He sighed and walked to the bed, putting the tray down on the bedside table. "Don't start, Lana."

"You did, didn't you?" She tugged on his arm, the movement causing her to hiss in pain. "You don't understand."

He placed his hand over hers, the bandage rough under his palm. "I understand you didn't have to go through this."

"Oh yes I did!" She was becoming agitated, her legs moving

restlessly under the covers.

He sat down on the edge of the bed and tried to calm her down. "Do you think this was worth it?"

"Yes!"

He gave her an ibuprofen, holding the milk for her while she swallowed it down. "No. Seeing you in pain isn't worth it."

Her brow furrowed, her lips thinned, and her eyes flashed up at him. "I would rather go through this, knowing I'll heal, than have you *dead,* you stubborn son of a bitch."

"Hey. Mom doesn't like to be called that."

It worked; her eyes rolled, but her body relaxed. "You know what I mean, wolfman. No way could I live with you dead." She grabbed hold of him again, ignoring her own pain. "I can't lose you."

"You won't."

"You were bleeding so much." She was beginning to cry.

"Shh." The hell with Annabelle. Chris carefully pulled Lana into his arms. "I'm here. Cole's gone. You're safe now."

He was surprised when she punched him in the arm. "Idiot."

"What?"

"Get it through your thick skull! You. Almost. *Died!*"

"Ow." She'd pinched him, hard. "Okay, okay. I get it. But why you?"

"You think men are the only ones who can ride to the rescue?"

He decided not to answer on the grounds that he might be incinerated.

Lana glared up at him impatiently. "I thought so. If I had been the one on the ground and Zach reached for you, what would you have done?"

He didn't even hesitate. "Whatever was necessary."

"Because...?"

Because I love you. He blinked. A slow smile spread across his face. He'd never felt so happy in his entire fucking life, not even when his mark had appeared on her skin. "You love me."

"Duh."

"Duh? The best you can say is duh?" He held back the urge to tickle her, to force her to say what he already knew.

She held her hand to his cheek. "We both do."

He gulped. "We?" His hand immediately went to her stomach.

"Huh?" Her eyes went wide. "No! Not that. Zach."

"Oh." He was more disappointed than he'd expected. "I guess we'll have to try harder, then."

It was her turn to gulp. "Harder?"

"Mm-hmm." He held a grape to her lips, teasing her with it. "*Much* harder."

"Oh boy."

He chuckled and slipped the grape between her lips. "Say it for me."

She swallowed the grape. "You first."

Not a problem. He wanted to shout it from the highest rooftop, post it to his Facebook, hell, he'd put it on the front page of Black Wolf Designs if he could. "I love you, little witch."

"I love you too, wolfman."

When he kissed her, she tasted of grapes and the sweetness that was his witch.

Chapter Twenty-Four

Lana picked at the bandage on her hand. She'd been bedridden for two weeks now, and finally Grammy was going to let her get up. She was still in some pain, but between her grandmother's nursing and Chris's attentiveness, she was mostly healed.

Davis Godwin was now officially listed as a warlock in The Registry, along with two other members of the Godwin family, including his second son, Paul, and his daughter, Genevieve. The only odd thing was Genevieve had called Chris to personally apologize for the actions of her family members, and to offer reparation for their injuries. Neither of them had been willing to accept her offer, and she'd left it at that.

Lana had no idea what the younger woman was up to, but there'd been something strange about her. Something Lana almost wanted to trust. But until they could figure out how Cole and his father had tampered with The Registry, she was unwilling to trust her instincts on where this particular Godwin was concerned. She had no idea if Genevieve had attempted to contact any of the other Becketts.

"Ready, sweetheart?"

She blinked up at Chris, pulled out of her thoughts. "More than."

He looked at Grammy, who nodded. "Any sign of serious

pain and you're back on the bed, young lady."

Lana stuck out her tongue and put her hands in Chris's. "Pull, He-Man."

With a muffled laugh, Chris pulled.

Lana stood. Her legs were wobbly, but there was very little pain. "I'm good." It felt great to be on her own two feet. Chris had been forced to carry her everywhere; just trying to place weight on her legs had caused excruciating pain. The first time they'd tried she'd actually screamed. "Can we take the bandage off my hand now?"

Chris held her steady while she made her way to the gold wing chair he'd moved from the great room into the bedroom. "Let's get you settled in first, okay?"

The chair was looking better and better. "Sure."

Chris helped her to sit. Her legs were shaking like leaves, letting her know her recovery was going to be a lot longer than she'd thought. It was disappointing, to say the least. "You did good, sweetheart."

He was grinning, but she could see the strain the last couple of weeks had put him under. Dark circles ringed his eyes, and it looked like he might have lost some weight. She'd had to beg him to go running more than once, just so his wolf could get out for a while. "Thanks." She began picking at the bandage again. The scar underneath was itching like a son of a bitch. "Can we get this off now?"

Grammy frowned and moved forward. "Does it hurt?"

"No, but the itching is driving me nuts."

Grammy's face blanked. "Itching?"

Uh-oh. That look on Grammy's face never boded well. "Um, yes."

Grammy took a deep breath. "Let's take a look, shall we?"

Grammy reached for Lana's hand, and the itch turned to a searing burn. "Ow!"

"What?"

"It burns!" Lana snatched her hand away, and the burn immediately diminished. "What the fuck?"

"Alannah!"

Lana grimaced. "Sorry, Grammy."

"Let me." Chris reached for her hand, and Lana let him take it, waiting for the burn.

It didn't come. It still itched, but it didn't burn. "It doesn't hurt, but the itch is still there." In fact, with Chris's touch the itch had increased.

Grammy was looking worried. "Unwrap it, please."

Chris pulled the bandage off carefully. "Holy shit."

Grammy didn't bother yelling at him for the curse. Everyone was too busy staring at Lana's palm.

There, in the center of her palm, was the shadow of a wolf. "What the hell?" She'd known the outline of a wolf had been burned into her palm from the protection amulet, but that's all it had been, an outline. Now the outline had been filled in, the black fur almost visible, the eyes a searing gold. And it itched worse than ever.

"I need to call Zach, find out if he has any idea what's happening." Chris reached for the phone and dialed a number. "Zach? Get back to me as soon as you get this, okay? Something odd is going on with Lana's scar."

"Grammy?"

"Hmm?" Grammy was studying the wolf, careful not to touch Lana's hand. Lana stared at it as well.

Suddenly she *knew* who the wolf was. "I think Gareth is in trouble."

"Why do you say that, sweetheart?" Chris returned to her side, his expression concerned.

She shrugged. "Instinct."

Chris picked up the phone. "I'll call him now." He put it on speaker when Gareth answered. "Listen, Lana thinks you're in trouble."

"Um. I wouldn't call it *trouble*, precisely."

"What would you call it?"

"Having an 'oh shit' moment?"

Chris rubbed the bridge of his nose. "Gareth."

"Maybe FUBAR would be a better description."

Lana hobbled toward to the bed. "Gareth?"

"Hey, Lana!" He sounded pleased to hear her voice. "How'd you know something was wrong?"

"You know the scar on my palm?"

"Yes," Gareth drawled.

"It looks like you."

Chris growled. His wolf was getting all possessive again. "Really?"

She kicked him in the shin. Seriously, if she didn't get him to calm down, he'd wind up peeing a circle around her or something. "Down, boy."

Gareth coughed. "So your scar looks like me?"

She made a face. "Okay, maybe it doesn't look exactly like you, but it *feels* like you."

"Huh."

"So, anything going on with you recently?"

Gareth sighed. "Kind of."

"Gareth."

"I just got a call from the court."

Chris was frowning, but suddenly Lana knew. "Congratulations."

"You're fucking kidding me, right?" Gareth sounded outraged. "Me? King?"

Chris looked like someone had poked him in the ass with a stick. "What?"

"The council just called and told me the king had named *me* his heir. What the fuck is up with that?"

Chris started laughing.

"This is not funny. If it was Daniel, maybe. Zach, definitely. Me? Not. *Funny.*"

Chris just laughed harder.

"What kind of king would I make, anyway? The kind that sucks big fat hairy moose balls, that's what kind."

By now Chris was laughing so hard he wasn't making a sound.

Lana tried to be supportive, but it was hard when she was holding back her own laugh. "I think you'll make a great king."

"No offense, babe, but you've never sat in on a wizard's court before. Trust me. I'll be craptastic at it."

Lana waved her hand, forgetting Gareth couldn't see it. "It can't be *that* bad. And *don't* call me babe."

There was silence for a moment. "Trust me. It will be *bad.*"

"Can you turn it down then?"

"Sure I can. And right afterward I can declare myself the Emperor of Never-Never."

"Once the king declares his heir, unless something happens to said heir, he's kind of stuck with it." Chris wiped his eyes and sighed. "Gareth is the future king whether he likes it or not."

Lana nudged Chris with her elbow and smirked. *"Your future king, wolfman."*

Chris groaned. "Aw, crap."

"Y'know, you're right. I *will* be Chris and Daniel's boss, won't I?" She could practically hear Gareth rubbing his hands together with glee.

"Oh now, wait a minute—"

Gareth rolled over Chris's sudden objection. "This could have some unexpected perks." Gareth cackled gleefully "Oh yeah, I can see some side benefits to having built–in minions."

"Asshole."

"That's *King* Asshole to you, minion."

Lana's palm itched. "Gareth, be careful, okay? I'm worried something might happen now they've declared you the heir."

"Your palm still itching?" All of the playfulness had left Gareth's voice. Suddenly she was listening to the overprotective Gareth she'd first met. "Could there be any danger to you or the rest of the family?"

She felt her mouth open, but nothing came out. For some reason, the words *you or the rest of the family* brought home she really was a part of the Becketts now in a way that hadn't hit her before. "I think most of the danger is directed at you this time."

"This time?"

Aw crap. The last time Gareth had sounded like that, she'd wound up kneeing him in the balls. "I'll let you know if I think it's going to change. For now, watch your back."

"Will do. Thanks for the heads up."

"You're welcome. Your Highness."

She giggled when he sighed. "Do me a favor. Make plans to head to New York for about a week. I'll need some family around me when I go to the court."

Chris answered for them both. "Will do, bro. Be careful."

"I will. Bye."

Chris hung up the phone. "Wow. King Gareth."

The eyes of the wolf changed to blue. "Zach."

"Zach?"

"The wolf's eyes turned blue." She held out her hand and showed him the mark.

"Aw crap." Chris flopped onto the bed next to her. Chris's jaw clenched. "Hell. Now what?"

"Now I leave you two alone for a bit." Grammy headed for the bedroom door. "I'll try and find out where Zach is and make sure he's all right." She pointed to Lana. "You. Get some rest." She pointed to Chris. "You. Make sure she rests."

"Yes, ma'am." Chris saluted, but it lacked some punch considering he was flat on his back.

Grammy left with a sigh, closing the door behind her.

"You think Zach is okay?"

Lana looked down at Chris. "It doesn't have the urgency Gareth's itch did, so yeah, I think he's okay for now."

He relaxed into the bedding. "Thank the Lord. I'm not sure I can deal with any new surprises right now."

She lowered herself to lie next to him, grateful the movement was relatively pain free. "No more surprises. Gotcha."

He took her hand into his, stroking her fingers. "With Gareth as heir, things are going to change."

"For the Becketts, anyway."

He turned his head and stared at her. "You're part of this

family now. That means things will change. I doubt Gareth will sit still for someone making comments about witches when his sister-in-law is one."

"And his brother." Although she was no longer certain *witch* was the appropriate label for Zach. She was pretty sure it was something...more, but until she was certain? Her lips were zipped shut.

"True." He rolled over onto his side, resting his head on his palm. His other hand landed on her thigh and began rubbing in slow circles. "You know, Annabelle said you needed to rest."

The building heat in his eyes had butterflies dancing in her stomach. "Yes she did."

"And she said I should make *sure* you rested."

His hand was beginning to creep up her leg. Her pussy clenched in anticipation of his touch. It had been so long since they'd made love. "Uh-huh."

"Feeling tired?" He cupped her through her pajama pants, kneading her, stroking her, the thin cotton no real barrier between them.

"Not at all." He stood up and maneuvered her so that her head was on the pillow, sliding her pajamas off until she was completely naked. "How did you know?"

He pulled his T-shirt over his head with a grin. "Instinct."

Lana settled against the pillow and watched her mate get undressed. She put her hands behind her head and smiled when her fingertips brushed the shadow of the wolf. And when the real thing crawled into bed, his golden eyes gleaming, she welcomed him with open arms.

About the Author

Dana Marie Bell wrote her first short story when she was thirteen years old. She attended the High School for Creative and Performing Arts for creative writing, where freedom of expression was the order of the day. When her parents moved out of the city and placed her in a Catholic high school for her senior year, she tried desperately to get away, but the nuns held fast, and she graduated with honors despite herself.

Dana has lived primarily in the Northeast (Pennsylvania, New Jersey and Delaware, to be precise), with a brief stint on the US Virgin Island of St. Croix. She lives with her soul mate and husband, Dusty, their two maniacal children, an evil, ice-cream-stealing cat and a bull terrier that thinks it's a Pekinese.

You can learn more about Dana at www.danamariebell.com or contact her at danamariebell@gmail.com.

To save the woman he loves, he must push his gifts to the brink.

Cynful

© 2012 Dana Marie Bell
Halle Shifters, Book 2

Julian DuCharme, a rare Spirit Bear with legendary healing powers, is finally free from the threat of death, finally free to claim his mate—but she's not having it. While his Bear screams it's time to mate, the love of his life wants to date.

Holding his Bear in check while convincing her he's not out to control her won't be easy. She's stubborn and a closeted geek—in other words, perfect for him.

Cynthia "Cyn" Reyes, owner of Living Art Tattoos, thinks Julian is the hottest thing on two legs. That doesn't mean she's going to roll over for his masculine charm. She watched her mother flounder when her father passed away, and she's determined to never lose herself to someone else. Not even a man who would jump the moon for her, if she asked that of him.

When the women of Living Art are targeted by a killer, Julian doesn't think twice about pouring out his last drop of power to keep Cyn safe. But it's Cyn who'll give up everything—her independence, even her humanity—to keep a terrifying vision from coming true.

Warning: This novel contains explicit sex, graphic language, a tattooed heroine and the Bear who loves her. Maybe he'll finally convince her to tattoo him with "Property of Cyn".

Available now in ebook and print from Samhain Publishing.

Haunted by personal betrayal, stalked by a murderer and taunted by destiny. Finding justice—not to mention a little faith—has never been so hard.

Wrath

© *2011 Denise Tompkins*
The Niteclif Evolutions, Book 2

A murderer is terrorizing the streets of London, targeting women who look suspiciously like Maddy. Under the mantle of darkness, the killer attacks his victims from behind, severing their heads with startling efficiency and single-minded brutality. A single gold coin is left at the scene of every crime, buried in the neck of each victim. Nothing adds up, and the deeper Maddy gets into the investigation, the more she learns that there are hostile eyes in every faction—some malicious, others murderous.

Amid her struggles to stop a seemingly unstoppable killer, Maddy learns that dreams are far too fragile to juggle. Her newfound love is crumbling around her under the burdens of guilt and blame, and where one man abandons her, another is slated by the gods to take his place. Defiant, Maddy finds her struggles with free will versus destiny have only just begun.

Figuring out whom she should trust, and when, will force Maddy to reassess her alliances...and reaffirm her fragile mortality.

Warning: Contains Scottish and Irish brogues, heads that—literally—roll, seriously random acts of violence, heartbreak and hope, explicit m/f sex in a variety of locations, a voyeuristic vampire and one dinner table that will never be the same.

SAMHAIN
PUBLISHING

www.samhainpublishing.com

Green for the planet.
Great for your wallet.

PUBLISHING

It's all about the story...

Romance

HORROR

ROMANCE

www.samhainpublishing.com